# AUTHORIZED CRUELTY

a novel

## JANICE BARRETT

blue denim press

*Authorized Cruelty*

Published by Blue Denim Press Inc.
First Edition
ISBN -978-1-927882-91-7

This is a work of fiction. Although the novel covers historical incidents and important political and military figures at the time, the story is fictitious.

Cover Image—Terrie Frankel
Cover Design—Shane Joseph
Library and Archives Canada Cataloguing in Publication:
Title: Authorized Cruelty: a novel / Janice Barrett.
Names: Barrett, Janice (Dramatist), author.
Description: First edition.
Identifiers: Canadiana (print) 2023049160X | Canadiana (ebook) 20230491626 | ISBN 9781927882917
   (softcover)    |    ISBN    9781927882924    (Kindle)    |    ISBN 9781927882931 (EPUB) | ISBN 9781927882948
   (IngramSpark EPUB)
Subjects: LCSH: Vietnam War, 1961-1975—Fiction. | LCGFT: Novels.
Classification: LCC PS8603.A7689 A95 2023 | DDC C813/.6—dc23

# Dedication

This book is dedicated to the approximately 11,000 American women who participated in the Vietnam war. Ninety percent of the women were nurses. Fifty-nine American women (eight nurses and the rest were volunteers, including four POWs) died during the Vietnam war.

It is also dedicated to my sister Paddy Barrett who has battled all her life to survive Neurofibromatosis type 1. She is a warrior with incredible spirit.

What readers are saying about *Authorized Cruelty*

"Barrett weaves threads of her own ancestry into this riveting story of a woman's grueling marathon to survive a man's war, compromised by political and family expectations. I couldn't put it down." **Yvonne Van Lankveld, author of** *The Park Street Secrets.*

"*Authorized Cruelty* is an intense look at a turbulent time in America. Barrett's engaging characters and vivid details are authentic and haunting. A well-researched, provocative examination of the Vietnam War's destructive effect on humanity."
**Sharon Frayne, award-winning author of** *The Sound of a Rainbow.*

"Loved the book, a very enjoyable read. As an anti-war teenager in the late 60's I could relate to Patty's views, fears and anger. The writing created a clear picture of Vietnam and the political climate. I would recommend this to both book clubs that I belong in."
**Avid reader, Darlene Roos, retired Travel Professional.**

"Strap on your boots and hang on tight. Janice Barrett gives the reader a unique perspective in this fast-paced novel full of history snapshots, which turn the story on its heels in every chapter."
**Barbara Baker author of** *Summer of Lies* and *What about me?*

"In this fast-paced novel, Barrett takes readers on a harrowing journey through the jungles of war and government corruption." **Author Margery Reynolds.**

"A devastatingly truthful work of fiction. Fast-paced. An unflinchingly descriptive blend of fact and fiction told through the eyes of a courageous, resourceful young woman caught in the jungles of the war in Viet Nam." **Sylvia Barnard, author of** *Rhubarb, Strawberries, and Willows.*

# Prologue

Four months into his tour of duty in Vietnam, Christopher Fielding was looking forward to this ceasefire and didn't mind that precipitation made clothes cling to the body. His army fatigues acted like a cool compress against the fevered noon-day sun. A backhand swipe cleared away fat raindrops hanging from the end of his nose. He had a poncho, but wouldn't wear it. The rubberized material would soak him in sweat, worse than fresh rain. Besides, it was noisy when the deluge hit.

Wrestling each boot from the mud's suction grip, he felt the weight of water canteens and ammo shift in his rucksack. The exertion reminded him of being back home in a gym doing leg presses. He wasn't looking forward to the downpour stopping because that meant swarming mosquitoes and ants. Even with his boots done up, mud sucked in and spewed out with each step. He stopped along the creek bank and watched the drops bounce on the water like black blisters percolating.

The muffled spit of gunfire penetrated the static of rain. A thump hammered hard into his shoulder knocking the wind out of him. Sprawled in the mud, he snorted to keep the water out of his nostrils. He laid face down, blowing bubbles between sputters of breath before his brain commanded his head to turn. He didn't feel pain. The bullet must have missed. He was alright. A gush of warmth soaked his skin. Bright red flowed from shoulder down the line of his arm. Christopher thought of the white chalk outline police drew around a dead body.

The water rippled as his assailant splashed through the shallow creek towards him. With rifle slung around his back, Christopher was at his foe's mercy. He said a prayer as the gook took aim. Grabbing the submerged sandaled foot, forgetting about the pain in his shoulder, Christopher hoisted up and away, knocking his adversary backward. Without boots to weigh him down, he was on top now and bent the enemy's arm until the sickening snap was heard. The revolver splashed into the water. He knelt on the aggressor's arm, feeling through the mud and water for the weapon, knowing the screams were too high-pitched to be a man's. With the revolver in hand, it was his turn to play God. It struck him that he had a choice. He had never considered any other option but "shoot to kill." He didn't know if he had any pity left in him.

Christopher took his eyes away for a second to locate his rifle. It was plugged with mud, and could fail to fire. He had never killed a woman before. At least, not that he knew of. He watched her tiny frame shake, unsure if the mud streaks running down her face were cleaned by tears or rain. They were face-to-face, and he had been her, just minutes ago. And the prayer he had said for mercy had not yet been licked off his lips. It was his turn, not to pray for mercy, but to offer it. She looked about the same age as his sister, Patty.

Suddenly, he was tired of being numb, and afraid to feel, tired of seeing corpses bagged, tagged, and shipped to become nothing more than inconvenient paperwork. Without having to look inside a body bag, he could tell by the smell whether it was a fresh kill, and by the shifting weight if the corpse was whole or in pieces. The bodies had stopped being sons, brothers, and husbands, and were only numbers to be meticulously recorded for the butcher's bill, so that statistical reports and ratios could be compiled.

"It's your lucky day." He holstered his revolver. The sole of his boot stuck out of the water and he went over to put it on, re-shouldering his rifle.

The single shot was loud and unexpected. Blood gurgled up Christopher's throat, making his tongue convulse. He should have known better than to heed his emotions. He had forgotten the rule of the game known since childhood: if you get me, I'll get you back, even harder. There was enough time to get a shot off. But he chose not to. Christopher dropped to his knees. The rifle was heavy on his back as he slumped into the water. No more bubbles floated in the red stream.

# Chapter 1

I buried myself today. Only half a person left. I should be there with him—tucked into his arms forever. His love never to be felt again. His strength sapped from me. A hollow shell of who I should be. Memories that can't caress or soothe. No one left who knows me as well.

I hug Soko's pillow, hoping for a scent of him. My sorrow mimics the emptiness of his side of the bed. Then I laugh, thinking about the time he asked me what twerking was. I was the cool one, so he didn't question me when I said, "twerking is a person who tweets." We both laughed when we saw Miley Cyrus twerking with Robin Thicke at the MTV Video Music Awards.

Forcing myself out of bed, I go to the kitchen and make coffee. Soko was always up before me and had it made and waiting. Turning the radio on, I walk to the computer. I feel like a Luddite when it comes to technology and the lingo. Browser—Wowser, what's that?

For a decade, I treated my computer like a new-fangled typewriter. It was eleven years ago, I discovered Google and Facebook. In my generation, we believed what we were told as truth. Now, I know differently. The words, "this site can't be reached," popped up on the computer. "Don't get your panties in a bunch," I say to the screen, clicking the refresh button.

I like to surf the internet. What strange words kids have for things. How would someone think to put surfing and the internet together? How would that make sense? But how does anything today?

Looking at an ad for a beaten-up vintage lighter, I wipe away a tear. I'd seen so many of these lighters in Vietnam but with different inscriptions on them. But this one, I'd never seen before. It told the whole story simply. Engraved into this Zippo lighter are the words, *We the unwilling, led by the unqualified, to kill the unfortunates, die for the Ungrateful.*

I saw the remains of villages set ablaze. Zippo lighters were used to light flamethrower tanks when their built-in, electrical igniters didn't work. To put those words on a lighter used to destroy villages and burn people to death was unimaginable. Feeling a tightness in my chest, I try to hold back the tears. How could anyone reconcile their actions with those words?

The lighter is for sale for over four hundred dollars. Before I click on "buy," I research further. I've learned to be skeptical. It is supposedly written by an unknown soldier. All this money and no lawsuits by someone claiming to be the author! Or the inheritor if the author was deceased. Someone's raking in paydirt when they didn't even write this. One reliable site claims this was the motto for many soldiers during the Vietnam war. Another site, just as reliable, debunks the motto and says it is a modern art piece made to look vintage.

Soko would know. I turn my head looking down the hall as if expecting him to walk into the kitchen. Then I remember. And continue my search. Konstantin Josef Jirecek a Czech historian and diplomat (1854-1918) wrote similar words to these.

Meanwhile, the quote is in books, on T-shirts, and is a thriving money maker. Designed to capitalize on heartbreak. So many opinions to weed through. Misinformation spreads like an uncontrolled wildfire on social media. Everyone argues their version of the truth. No one knows the truth anymore.

In my generation, I protested, but no one questioned the information we were given that formed our opinions, not like today. Fake news is the buzzword. How naive we were until, January 30,

1968, the day the government was found out. Lies, so many lies, and secrets.

\*\*\*

White House officials told the American people they were winning the war in Vietnam and that the US troops might soon be withdrawn. This was the first war televised straight from the battlefield, unedited, to television sets. Tokyo transmitted these satellite broadcasts and brought the American public the real truth. The North Vietnamese simultaneously attacked thirty-eight major cities, hitting almost every major US military installation. They invaded thirteen of the sixteen provincial capitols. The attacks happened during a ceasefire.

Citizens sat in front of their TV trays eating dinner and watching the six o'clock news, stunned to see fighting taking place on the grounds of the US embassy in Saigon. Many people were afraid that President Johnson would call for an escalation of troops. The younger generation wasn't willing to fight in this war when there was no imminent danger to the USA.

While eating mom's apple pie, millions of Americans witnessed, their ally, South Vietnamese police chief Colonel Loan, put his gun to the head of a man and fire. It was like a mob hit. The guy had his hands tied behind his back. He was wearing a plaid shirt and shorts, not a North Vietnamese uniform, and Loan shot him in broad daylight in front of the cameras.

That went against everything that American society stood for. And the USA was backing them! It wasn't just one bad apple because the camera panned around the crowd. The American people saw their allies grinning and laughing as they looted North Vietnamese corpses. How could Americans say the South Vietnamese were the good guys? With that telecast of the Tet Offensive, the people knew they had been lied to by their government. And their loved ones in Vietnam had been unprepared, feeling safe under the guise of a ceasefire.

\*\*\*

As part of the USO tour, Patty's territory was I Corp, in the northern part of South Vietnam. This area was called the backdoor or asshole of the country. No one wanted to be assigned here, but it was close to where her brother Christopher was stationed in Da Nang. I Corp was mandatory initiation for all USO rookies before they could earn the right to come through the front door of III Corp around Saigon that was reserved for the veteran performers. Like the army, rank had its privileges.

Patty had been told that if she faced her fears they would go away. No matter how many times she flew in a helicopter, her fear of heights persisted. The noise on take-off hurt her ears and she didn't know if she shook from vibration or fear. The smell of fuel plugged her nose, and the whirl of rotor blades made her hunch forward, fighting gusts of wind that twisted hair into tangled knots.

The sun and the shadowed clouds painted a color swatch of green hues, dappling the treetops to look like a tropical paradise—its beauty deceitful. A picture postcard from hell. At this safe distance, ants didn't swarm to drink the liquid in her eyes, and bugs didn't bite and sting, and men weren't tortured to death.

Squished against Jackie, Patty felt secure on the canvas seat.

"Air pocket." The pilot's warning came too late.

Jackie's lipstick slipped from her grasp and rolled over the bumpy aluminum floor. It pitched between the rivets. Luckily the clutter of microphones and accordions corralled it. Jackie leaned out of her seat. Without a body to crowd her, Patty felt anxious. She took out a transistor radio and put earphones in to distract from the fear. She didn't know why Jackie bothered with lipstick when no amount of color could add warmth to her "beauty queen contestant" smile.

The tempo to *Daydream Believer* was lost in Patty's heavy breathing, with her heartbeat pounding louder than the bass. The music was interrupted by a special announcement.

"We have some bad news for you marines out there," a modulated voice said through the earphones of the transistor radio. "Looks like there is no Santa after all," declared the radio announcer for the United States Armed Forces. "The ceasefire which started today, the thirtieth of January 1968, for Tet, the Vietnamese New Year, has officially been canceled. Effective immediately, all forces will resume intensified operations and troops will be placed on maximum alert. For the allied forces across the republic, it will be business as usual."

The announcement suddenly made this trip redundant. They had to go back, at least for now, Patty realized.

Jackie snatched the lipstick just as the pilot started his descent.

Bracing for "Huey" the helicopter's thunk, Patty's feet pressed into the floor of the huge iron hawk. Dirt sprayed when the bird landed, and the pilot shut off the engine.

Patty hollered over her shoulder to the pilot. "The ceasefire's been canceled. Take us back to Saigon."

The pilot leaned out of his seat. "Get out. I'm not a taxi."

She gripped the woven canvas strips behind her head. "I'm not leaving."

"My orders were to deliver the two of you here."

Patty looked out at the crowd of marines outside waiting for them. "I don't care about your orders. It's not safe. Fly us back to Saigon."

The pilot shifted his bulk out of his seat and strutted toward her. "That's not part of my flight plan. And it's not your nickel paying the meter."

Patty hated the army. Orders superseded common sense. The pilot seized her arm and shoved her toward the door, knocking her into Jackie, who was gripping her duffle bag.

"Let go of me," she snarled jerking her arm.

She tripped over equipment losing her balance, but he tightened his grip to prevent the fall. When he delivered her to the door gunner, releasing his hold, Patty crooked an elbow and brought it back, hitting his chest-plated armor. The door gunner clasped both her hands in his one hand and pulled her out of the chopper. With his other hand, he held her head down hunching her body; they ducked stone fragments and dirt spat by the spinning blades as they ran out from under the rotors.

"Get your hands off me." Patty twisted out of his grasp and turned as the pilot pitched her duffle bag out of the chopper.

The door gunner retrieved and dropped it at her feet. "What the hell's wrong with you? Why can't you be like your partner?"

Patty caught her shirt as it fluttered up to offer a peep show. "Where is your base commander?"

"He's coming." The door gunner nodded his head toward an older man who was clearing a path that closed behind him as quickly as he took his next step forward.

"Welcome young lady. I'm the C.O."

"Do you realize…" Patty caught a glimpse of the door gunner's back as he walked away. "The ceasefire has been canceled!" She had to scream above the crowd. "We have to get back to Saigon."

The C.O. smiled as if she hadn't spoken at all.

"We have to get back on the Huey."

Crooking his arm in hers, he walked her away from the chopper. His breath, stale and reeking of whiskey, wheezed from behind tobacco-stained teeth. He was so close, she was drowning in the smell, held down by that aged spotted arm that pulled on her tense body. She knew enough about the army to know not to make a scene. Not in front of the men.

Patty tried to ignore the cajoling and laughter of the group as Jackie strolled passed them and went down the hill. She heard Jackie gasp as her feet slid on the damp grass, threatening to send her sprawling forward. Three marines caught her before she lost balance, and, from then on, she had a marine on each arm, just the way she liked it.

From this vantage point, the full length of the camp was visible. Concertina wire surrounded it, and armed sentries guarded the gate. The C.O. guided her to the bottom of the hill. On the right was a motor pool with trucks, tanks, and jeeps lined up like a used car lot. A canopy had been erected beside it so mechanics could work on the vehicles in the rain. The air stunk of gasoline and engine oil. As they walked by, a greasy mechanic in a dirty undershirt and pants slid out from underneath a truck and whistled at her. Wrench in hand, another marine poked his head out from under the hood of a jeep and stared.

The marine base was laid out grid-like with tents lined up on either side of a wide dirt road. A foot above the ground, twelve-inch-wide planks, in eight-foot lengths, had been raised and provided a walkway that led to a wooden platform. Surrounded by sandbags, a tent occupied much of the platform.

The C.O. steered her toward it, away from the group. "We'll talk in my office."

An American flag hung limp on a pole in front of the tent. The C.O. held the door flap open for Patty. Although there was no fresh air to let in, large canvas window flaps were still open on all sides, exposing mosquito netting.

"Please have a seat." The C.O. pulled out a chair for her, then settled into a wooden chair across the desk and lit up an unfiltered Salem. "Now, isn't this better?" Ashes circled the ashtray, speckling the cluttered paperwork in front of him.

Patty pulled out a roll of breath mints, offering him one.

He moved in closer and smiled. "No thanks."

Although his cigarette was menthol, it did nothing to help his breath.

He flicked the ashes near the ashtray. "Your friend seems to be enjoying herself."

"She's so busy doing her, 'look at me; aren't I beautiful' thing, that if the enemy landed in her lap, the only thing she'd notice was that her audience got bigger."

Phlegm rumbled in the C.O.'s chest as he choked back a laugh.

Patty moved in closer and placed both arms on his desk. "I'm not here to go to war. I want the war to end."

The C.O. hunched over in his chair, with head shadowing a large map of Vietnam he pulled out of the desk drawer. The chair's casters scraped the cheap flooring and squeaked with his shifting weight. A round, battery-operated clock clicked off the minutes while he returned to searching in the drawer.

"I want to know what the army is doing sending us out here to entertain the troops when the ceasefire has been canceled?"

He acted like she wasn't there; looked right past her. She knew the game. Her father had played it often enough. Make them wait to show them who's boss. She didn't have the patience to out-grin him.

"What's the matter? Lose something?" The sarcasm in her voice was evident. She would torment him into talking.

Trying to blow a tiny piece of tobacco off the white coating on his tongue, he stuck it out and then quickly sucked it back in, spitting air across it. Finally, after several tries, he gave up and scraped it off with his index finger, then rubbed his thumb and finger together.

*How gross. Not shaking hands with him.* "Try and retrace your steps. Sometimes that helps." She would make him feel like a bumbling fool, looking for something that they both knew wasn't there.

His nose was the first part of his face to change to a purple pink. "I don't know who the hell you think you are, but I give the orders here. You sit there and speak when you are spoken to. In case you don't know, I'm the one who determines what you do or don't do." He leaned forward, a protruding vein in his forehead throbbing. "You will leave here only when I say you can."

"Does this mean you've found what you're looking for?" Patty didn't shrink from his glare. She leaned back and relaxed in the chair. Her feet were planted on the floor, legs comfortably apart. She couldn't be intimidated by him or his rank.

The raucous laughter outside was the precursor to their dilemma.

"You can tell by all the hoopla outside that the men have been eager for you girls to get here. They all worked together preparing for your arrival because that's what army life is like." His eyebrows rose to wrinkle his forehead and emphasize the importance of his words. "Teamwork—where every man works together, pulls his weight, does what he is trained for and what is expected of him."

Patty rolled her eyes. He should have had a pulpit in front of him the way he slammed down the sermon-like words to try and knock some sense into her. By the end, she wanted to raise her voice with a hallelujah, but stopped herself.

"My men have worked hard to accommodate you girls. I won't have them disappointed. Even the cooks were up extra early preparing a special lunch."

In a calm and pleasant voice, she said, "I'm not in the army. And I'm still waiting for an answer. How long have you known the ceasefire was canceled?"

His muscles flexed revealing a square jawline underneath folds of skin. "It takes months to organize the USO tour. Who goes where and when? You can't expect them to shut the whole operation down in an hour. It takes time."

His words came out in rapid fire, unlike the practiced sermon drawl. "So far today, the truce has been canceled for I and II Corp only. We just got the word ourselves because the South Vietnam government closed up shop early and forgot to tell us. You are in III Corp, so the cancellations don't directly concern you."

"What kind of bullshit is that? Of course, it concerns me when I'm on my way here."

"The truce for III Corp hasn't officially been canceled yet. And that's where you came from. The army notifies the personnel directly involved first. It's difficult enough just to figure out where people are, you can't expect them to know where you're going."

"That's why I have an itinerary, isn't it?"

Shades of purple-pink spread from his nose across his face and down his neck.

Patty sat forward in her chair. "According to army regulations, any American civilian visiting a military installation during wartime must be afforded maximum protection to ensure their safety. I want to know how you are complying with those regulations."

"So, you're the one; the general's daughter; the army brat who knows all about regulations. God, I'm glad I had sons. Your father must be proud of you!"

"I didn't come here to discuss my personal life with you."

"Then why did you come? To support the war effort?"

She bristled.

"If I had my way, you would have been blacklisted from the USO tour. You," he poked his finger at her, "are allowed to protest this war at home because my men are dying in this shithole to give you the right to freedom of speech."

"I didn't come here to support the war. I'm against it. My brother is against the war too, but he's a flag waver, so he felt obligated to fight it. I don't think people should die for something they don't believe in.

I'm against the war and the draft, not the men who feel obligated to fight it."

*Why was it so hard for people to see the difference? He would never get it.*

# Chapter 2

S tanding in the Chicago Airport that day in 1968, I didn't know it would change my life forever. We were Doves—against the war, fighting the Hawks who supported it. So many of us crammed into a cordoned-off section, corralled like animals in a pen. Our bodies close, and the smell of coffee, cigarette smoke, and body odor rubbing off on each other.

Protests were my thing back then. Colorful tie-dyed T-shirts competed with psychedelic swirls of red, purple, and blue on attention-getting signs. People screaming, their signs hammering out a beat for their words: *Hell No, We Won't Go.* The excitement. The crowd pushed us into each other. A girl jumped up beside me, waving a peace sign. *How Many More?* Voices were loud, overlapping, people struggling to make their signs more visible than the next. *Make Love Not War* was edged in flower power. A guy holding a sign as tall as himself read, *End the War Before It Ends You!* Juggling my sign and a cup of coffee, I pushed through the throng to see the returning soldiers.

Waving the sign above my head, I chanted the written words, "Stop the war in Vietnam, bring the boys home." My voice was drowned out by a group singing "What are you fighting for?" Mocked by the lyrics from Phil Ochs' song, the soldiers walked by while people gave them the middle finger, screaming "murderers," "baby killers." I was close enough to see the soldier's hurt and shocked expressions. They thought they were heroes. At least my brother did.

The tail end of my chant, "bring the boys…" fell off. *Home! Home to this?*

Murderers. The accusation grew with more voices. Baby killers. Their chant sickened me.

*My brother isn't a murderer.* I couldn't watch their reactions to the horrible name-calling. In a country divided, I had no side anymore. No place to express outrage at the war. I dropped my arms, and let the sign fall to the floor; my body wanted to do the same. I wouldn't be a part of any group that would treat my brother like this. I'd heard stories of returning vets being spat on but hadn't believed them. Now, I wondered if they were true. Many of the soldiers like Christopher were drafted. They didn't want to go. They risked their lives, slept in mud holes, and ate crap in a tin can to come home to this!

Walking out from behind the cordoned-off section, I shook hands with the first soldier I saw and said, "I'm glad you're home safe." I walked down the long line of soldiers and offered the same words. Since then, I'd been ostracized by my fellow anti-war protestors. They thought I was a Dove-turned-Hawk. I knew I was a good sister with an opinion about the politics of war.

I never thought less of my brother for going to Vietnam when he was against the war. Although I knew my dad would if he hadn't gone. And Christopher couldn't bear disappointing him. All his life, he looked up to Dad and tried to please him, but never could. This time, he would. He argued that serving his country was an obligation. A duty he wouldn't shirk. I was mad at him for not going to Canada with his friends who fled the draft. Sticking up for his beliefs was more important than our dad's idea of patriotism. But we each made our choices. When I got his last letter from Vietnam, I worried when he wrote, "You can lose who you are here; there's no normal."

\*\*\*

The C.O. lit another cigarette. "How can you protest the war and then join the USO tour? I have no tolerance for people like you who straddle the fence. You have no loyalty." His words spat and curled around the smoke. "You can't have it both ways. You're either for the war or against it, a Hawk or a Dove." He stuck his neck out, lips clamped in a sneer.

Patty shrunk back in the chair—tired of this same old debate. All the fight left her.

"The trouble with our country is that we've raised a generation of pansies who don't know how to stand up and fight for what's right. They want to make love and not war, and run off to Canada and hide from their responsibilities. If we didn't have the draft, we couldn't get enough people to support this war."

Feeling the fire ignite at those words, she leaned over the desk and pressed her hands on the wood. "That's right. So, you're saying the majority of people don't support this war? That's why the draft was needed. If we were a true democracy, we would listen to that majority, not use the draft, and not push for a war that the majority doesn't want."

The vein in the C.O.'s forehead pulsed, and grey hair stood out vividly against his pink scalp.

"It's hippies like you, who twist things around to suit your own purpose."

"And I shouldn't be discriminated against because of my beliefs. I have every right to be here. Doesn't democracy give people the right to disagree?" She leaned in closer inhaling his smoke. "If people are persecuted for saying what they think, isn't that communism? And aren't you here right now in Vietnam fighting the communists?" Her body shook and her voice became louder than she had intended. "*You* can't have it both ways." She sat back down and lowered her voice. "You can't be here fighting against communism, then take away my

democratic right to disagree with you. You're either for it or against it."
The words faded to a whisper.

"People like you are going to ruin our country for the rest of us."

"I didn't come here to debate the war. I do that at home. I came here to help entertain the troops, but I'm not risking my life for fifty dollars a day."

"You're not in danger. If I thought you were, I'd fly you out myself. I don't like what you stand for, but I'll protect your ass because I don't want to give those bleeding hearts back home anything more to protest about. And I won't see the army's reputation, or ability to protect visiting civilians, tarnished by the likes of you."

Patty's shoulders dropped. This was a "no-win" situation.

"Why are you so sure the enemy won't attack?"

"The communist government announced that there would be no shooting for the entire seven days. The Vietnamese have always honored a ceasefire. These people pay their respect to the dead during the Tet New Year, and it's considered a sacred time. I think someone is pushing the panic button." He ground out his cigarette in the ashtray, emphasizing his point. "We're bombarded with more FLASH priority, maximum alert, top secret hysterics than you can shake a stick at, and it's all meant to cover someone's political ass. My men have been looking forward to this show for a long time and I'm not going to take it away from them."

"And do the other bases feel the same?"

"Where is your next stop?"

"Camp Carroll."

He swiveled around to face the faded, soiled map. "We're here at Ca Lu on Route 9, now over here," his pen left a trail of red ink as he traced the road, "Twenty-two klicks west of us is Khe Sanh and, to the north, Camp Carroll at twenty klicks. But it's up to you girls. If you don't want to go on, it's your call."

The knots in her stomach began untangling.

"I'll have the orders changed and you'll be flown back tomorrow if that's what you want, after the show here. My lieutenant," his voice was raised loud enough to bring the man inside and to attention, "will take you to your quarters."

The lieutenant motioned with his hand toward the door. It was over like that. Patty was forced to stay at the base at least until tomorrow. It was the army's way of doing things. Her worries and concerns were dismissed as easily as a general can rid himself of a private.

She accompanied the lieutenant, feeling much like the defeated little girl she used to be when her father dismissed her opinions with a wave of his hand. Protesting the war was the only way she could be heard.

The Lieutenant led her out the door, and down the pathway. Tents were lined up on either side of a dirt road. Attracting attention, they picked up stragglers like the pied piper. As they walked past shower stalls, men whistled and waved. Some, with only a towel around their waist, joined the procession.

The narrowness of the road restricted the number of men who could walk side by side and squeezed out others to lag behind. Up ahead, it widened, allowing for vehicles to be parked next to a tent. When they heard moans in the distance, a marine beside her explained, "The meat factory is up ahead." Her stomach churned at his reference. She saw a sign for the field hospital.

Urinals and bedpans, propped up on sticks shoved into the ground, dried in the sun. Marines vying for Patty's attention shouted cat-calls as they walked by. The smell of coffee from the mess tent lingered, caught in the humidity. It was the usual questions, so predictable that they could have been scripted. Her answers, perfected over time, were like from a well-rehearsed skit.

One marine bullied his way to the front. "Where y'all from?"

Patty turned. "Washington."

"How long will you be here?" another piped up.

"I'm not sure." she continued walking.

"What's going on in the world?"

With her back to the men, Patty had no idea who spoke. She stopped and turned to address the crowd. "Nothing much. All the action is over here. But miniskirts are getting shorter."

A marine shouted "oorah!" The word echoed by every man sounded like a nearby roll of thunder and sent tingling waves through her body.

One marine at the back of the pack grumbled, "What did she say?"

"Stop shoving." The marine in front turned and shoved him back.

"I can't hear."

"I don't give a fuck."

"Knock it off, you two." The Lieutenant pointed at the instigators.

"Miss, can you speak a bit louder; it's hard to hear from back here."

Patty smiled, aware that she was a novelty since Nurses and Donut Dollies were rare this far north.

"So, what's a nice girl like you," the marine mopped up his sweaty forehead with the back of his hand, "doing in a place like this?"

*I've been waiting for that one.* "My agent told me, I was going to be the next big Hollywood bombshell. You guys know the army. All they heard was bombshell and thought I should be dropped here." She got the usual big laugh.

"Sis," a man hollered waving at Patty. It was Christopher's word. The word she cherished and prayed to hear again soon. Shielding her eyes from the sun, squinting into the brightness to make out the face that reminded her of her brother, she waited, choking back a lump in her throat, while he pushed through the crowd. She wished it was Christopher, even though she knew it was impossible. The questions stopped as the men noticed her distracted gaze.

"Sis," he said again wrapping his arms around her with a hug.

Before she was able to stop his embrace, he'd dropped his hands to his sides.

"I was beginning to think you'd never get here."

She couldn't resist his quirky grin. Stunned, she said nothing, curious about his next move.

"Come on guys, I haven't seen her in almost a year. We have catching up to do, personal stuff."

Some took the hint; others needed more convincing. "You know, Mom, Dad, the relatives; trust me, you'd be bored." He slapped the lieutenant on the shoulder, "I'll take my sister to her tent."

The Lieutenant took his cue from her affirmative nod and left with the others.

Just to be called sis again felt good. She couldn't stop smiling. Her brother Christopher was like him: unpredictable, anything for a joke. She'd nicknamed him "Prankster Gangster." He called her "Hammerhead" because of her stubborn serious nature. She missed that silliness in her life, missed him.

Two men remained behind. The soldier, whoever he was, stared them down and turned to Patty and said, "Mom said it was cancer." His bereaved look sent those last two die-hards on their way.

"That was a pretty low blow," Patty said.

"Trust me, they didn't feel a thing. They have the IQ of a green pepper."

"You're terrible."

"I call them like I see them." He held his hand out for a formal handshake. "Peter. Nice to meet you."

She shook his hand, "Patty. What am I supposed to say when they find out we're not related?"

"You'll be gone by then. So, how's the family?"

"Fine." The word was an automatic response.

"What about Uncle Jim's hernia operation?"

She covered her mouth before her giggle attracted more attention. "I don't believe you."

"You don't have to as long as everyone else does."

Peter guided her off the beaten path to skirt behind tents and other human activity. Camouflaged by an olive-green, cotton forest, they ducked under T-shirts, socks, underwear, and pants, thicker than leaves on trees, hanging from a makeshift clothesline.

Pushing Cammie's out of her way, she asked, "Are we in officer's quarters?"

Peter turned, his words slipping out between socks and underwear. "No, why?"

"The last time we stayed in officer's quarters, the marines didn't know we were in there and threw flaming bottles and other stuff at the tent."

"Morale's low."

"We had to wear flak jackets and helmets."

"Everyone knows which tent you're in, you're good."

They continued walking, popping in and out of overheard conversations.

"Here you are, home sweet home." Peter gestured with his arm to the door flap.

They stood outside the tent. Jackie's nasal voice penetrated through the canvas. "And I'm Miss Homecoming Queen and Miss Harvest. I nail the talent part in every competition. You'll see it at the show. When I get out of here, with this on my resume, I'll be a shoo-in for the bigger pageants. They like the patriotism thing, it's good for promotions. It's a whole industry."

Patty wasn't surprised by the one-sided chinwag. When Jackie spoke, there wasn't room for anyone else in her conversations. "You smell good. Not like the other guys. They could've at least showered and put deodorant on before they met us."

Peter lifted his arm to sniff his pit. "What do you think?"

She laughed. "I like Limburger cheese." They both laughed.

As Peter sauntered away, the end of the walkway scraped against the abutment of the tent's wooden platform that creaked and bounced under his weight. Patty unzipped the door flap and strolled in. She saw the surprised look on the marine who was inside, Jackie's nice-smelling man. He quickly made a lame excuse and left.

Clothes, make-up, and toiletries were strewn over Jackie's cot. The less-desirable cot shoved into the corner was empty. It never paid to be the last one in. Running shoes, socks, and dress shoes were scattered on the floor. It looked like they had been there for days instead of an hour.

Patty opened her duffle bag and took out make-up, footwear, and a red mini-dress. She kicked off her shoes and socks and dropped her heels on the floor. After a quick change, the girls headed out. Barely off the walkway, an entourage grew and led the way down a short path to the stage: the flat top of a bunker.

"That goes over here." Jackie strutted to the edge of the stage, smiling at a marine who was untangling the cord on the microphone.

"Would you mind giving me a hand with this mic?" Patty asked a short, stocky marine. "It goes in the center at the front of the stage, next to the other one."

For the sound test, Jackie went down to where the audience would be. She checked levels at different spots and then gave Patty two thumbs up when the sound was as good as it could be. It didn't take long for the Marines to invade when they heard the audio feedback. The grass in front of the stage disappeared as soldiers claimed their patch of land and waited for the show to begin. Some men sat and others lay on the grass, but all eyes were on the girls.

Ready to start the show, Jackie did her Miss Runway walk with the formal Queen's wave, flashing the front and back of her hand as she approached the microphone. Patty schlepped behind. Marines whooped and hollered as they stripped off their shirts and waved them above their heads when the music began. Jackie encouraged horseplay by blowing kisses, before picking up her accordion. They played The Beatles' "Penny Lane" while singing. The cheering, shouts, and whistles drowned out the notes as Patty struggled to stay on pitch. No one seemed to notice and, certainly, no one would complain if she was off-key. An ocean of bodies swayed in unison, and the music swelled like a tide when everyone sang the chorus to, "Happy Together" by The Turtles. A generator hummed behind the stage, its vibration running through their shoes.

Patty had performed in off-Broadway musicals. Over the last three months, she was getting used to the raw cat-calls of drunken and stoned men offering to "Light her Fire" at The Doors song. After their last number, "Respect" by Aretha Franklin, the applause turned to an encore plea that wasn't easily ignored. It resulted in extending their usual hour-long show. While Jackie captured the Marines' attention, Patty bowed out, grabbed her tape recorder, and exited the stage.

# Chapter 3

Patty ran into the trees behind the stage, retracing the route she had taken earlier with Peter. Most of the laundry was still on the lines. Her bright red mini-dress attracted men. *That's all I need. A parade of gawkers, like it's some sideshow.* Pilfering a shirt and pants, she put them on over her clothes and picked up her tape recorder.

When she heard a voice in a nearby tent say, "Jacks over deuces, read'em and weep," she ducked behind a tree. She was thankful the ground was hard, so her shoes didn't get stuck in it. No one exited the tent; she stepped back out. Next to a firepit, she found a helmet. She put it on, tucking her hair under it, then kept her head down. Trudging down the hard-packed dirt road, she was careful not to slip into the deep tire ruts. The banging of pots and pans became louder, so she knew she was headed in the right direction. She anticipated all the talking and yelling coming from the mess tent would lead to a decent meal.

There was no one around. The field hospital and the bedpans that had been drying in the sun were gone. Patty looked up at the jury-rigged fifty-gallon water barrel above where the operating room would be. She worried that the barrel and supports would give way and come down on her. Before she opened the flap and entered the tent, she batted at her pant legs creating a cloud of dust.

Trapped heat belched out the smell of human waste when she entered. An antiseptic scent acted like cheap perfume to mask the stink of urine that had been left to evaporate in bedpans. She looked down the row of ten cots on either side of the tent. Not all of them were filled, the worst cases would have been medevaced out.

Few men lifted their heads when she walked in. No one seemed interested in her until she lifted the helmet and shook free her long auburn hair. She shrugged out of the oversized shirt, dropped her pants, and revealed the red-hot mini dress.

"It's Christmas after all," a marine said, sitting up. He leveraged his weight on his hands and swung his legs off the edge of the cot.

Patty looked at his leg that was in a cast and asked, "Are you sure you should do that?"

"I feel so good, I could tap dance."

"Don't get up," she said.

He lifted his sheet and looked at his crotch. "Too late now."

*Some things would never change.* She put her heels back on.

One of the two medics on duty walked toward the marine. "No weight on that leg."

Patty looked at the medic. "I'm one of the USO entertainers. I thought if the men couldn't come to me, then I'd come to them."

He smiled. "The perfect medicine."

She went over to the patient closest to her. He didn't try to get up but smiled at her. "How are you doing?"

"Better now." Sweat beads glistened on his forehead, cheeks, and under his nose. Patty spotted a water jug on a stand in the middle of the tent, several glasses, and a stack of folded clothes on a shelf.

"What's your name?" she asked.

"Miles," he answered.

"Yeah," another marine yelled from across the room. "We've got Miles to go before we die." The place erupted with laughter.

She squeezed his hand. "Want some water?"

"That would be great."

Patty walked to the metal table. Hefting up the big water jug, she doused a cloth and poured water into a glass then carried them back to him.

Miles had propped himself up on his elbows, but she could tell the exertion was too much. She caught herself staring at the flattened sheet from his knees down. *Meat factory – slaughter house.* She tried not to think about crude words soldiers used and hoped he hadn't noticed her staring. Patty looked back at him to see if he was upset. His smile reassured her as she mopped his forehead. To take the strain off his arms, she raised his head, slid her body underneath, and cradled his head. She lifted his head and tipped the glass to his mouth. After he finished, she took the glass and slid out from under him.

"Water, water." A hoarse voice bleated. It was the marine who had made the joke about Miles. He was laying down now, his arm outstretched over the edge of the bed. *No doubt to cop a feel of my leg.* Walking over to him, staying out of his reach, she leaned over and handed him a glass of water. The other men roared with laughter. He sat up quickly and winced a bit, holding his side. Surgical gauze was wrapped around his waist.

"Come on, you can't blame a guy for trying," he said.

Patty walked back to the metal table and picked up a pencil and returned to his bedside.

"Ahh," he said, with arms outstretched for an embrace. "I knew you'd feel bad about being mean to me. Did you come to kiss and make up?"

Grabbing his medical chart at the end of his bed, she smirked while writing on it.

"What are you doing?" he asked.

"I'm recommending a barium enema." The men laughed. But the words she wrote were, "Speedy recovery and safe return."

"Does anyone want to hear a few songs?" she asked.

As expected, the men cheered. She got out her tape recorder. She had recorded the best of each song during rehearsals so she could sing along with them. Singing, moving from bed to bed, Patty held a hand, brushed a cheek, or ruffled hair.

In one of her brother's letters, Christopher had written that he wished he had a reminder of home. Home to her was her mother's touch. Since her mother's death, home had never felt the same. Her father wasn't a hugger and wouldn't let her cuddle next to him on the couch watching TV, as her mother would. He liked his space. She missed that closeness. That's why she offered comfort to these men. To give them a piece of home to hang onto. It was bizarre thinking. She didn't quite understand it, but she saw in their faces that touch made a difference. It somehow added humanity that was missing.

Coming up to the last bed on the right side of the tent, Patty stopped at a man who looked more like a boy. A picture of a woman about his age was on his lap next to a letter he was writing.

"Pretty girl." Patty pointed to the picture.

He licked his lips and ran his fingers through greasy hair while she sang "Happy Together." She pretended not to notice the dried semen stains before he covered them up with a sheet. The smell of excrement surrounded him, and he blushed when he saw her look over at the full bedpan. Embarrassed, she stepped back. Her shoulder knocked into an IV bag that dangled from a post. She turned and reached up to stop the swaying bag when her foot hit a dividing screen, knocking it over.

Behind it, the water barrel cast a shadow on the canvas roof. Four operating tables were sectioned off with privacy screens folded between them. Grey metal cabinets and shelves of supplies interspersed with IVs that dangled from posts and lined the back wall. A medic came up behind her.

"Sorry," Patty said.

"Not a problem." The medic picked up the screen that hid that area from the men.

Before heading up the other side of the tent, Patty squeezed the young marine's hand and moved to the next bed singing "Penny Lane."

A dark-haired man with olive-tanned skin had bandages covering his right eye, with black stitches that ran from his eye down to the corner of his mouth, and gauze taped over part of a tattooed snake that slithered across his chest.

"Are you Italian?" Patty asked.

He pinched his fingertips together and scrunched his hand. "I can fid yu wid a nice a pair of cement shoes," he offered in a heavy Brooklyn accent.

She kissed his forehead. He smoothed the sheet over himself and patted the bed inviting her to sit beside him.

"I don't get in bed that easy," she said between music beats, before moving on.

Even after three months, it was difficult not to react to the missing limbs and horrible disfigurements. Still, the marines smiled like everything was fine; like their futures hadn't been destroyed. And it was hard not to break down and cry.

She went up the row and ended in front of the man who had made fun of Miles. He reached for a cigarette, past a drawing of a nude woman. The nude's body was covered in numbered squares with many of them colored in. The caption read "Short Timers Chart." Wanting to light his cigarette, Patty picked up his Zippo lighter. She read the engraved words—*Screams and Suffering, Orders are Orders, No One Wins, Guilt Kills Slowly*. Her eyes opened as wide as her mouth.

He grabbed the lighter from her and lit his cigarette. She fought back tears; her breath heavy, finding it hard to get the air to sing the lyrics to "Respect." Her voice cracked with emotion when she sang, *all I'm askin' is for a little respect when you get home*. She knew when he got home, he'd be called a murderer and baby killer.

At the end of the song, she looked around and said, "I respect all of you for serving your country and want you back home soon. Take care and remember you're loved."

The marine beside her started the applause, and the rest joined in. Cheers resounded as she went over to the clothes she had left on the floor, dressed, tucked her hair back into the helmet, and walked to the door. The applause was louder as she walked out.

Patty couldn't get over the way the marine had snatched the lighter away. Concealing the words. Like it was a secret he didn't want to share. A reminder only for himself. Wanting to hide how he felt. Invisible pain. No one acknowledged it. Everyone thought them fine if they had all their limbs.

She looked back and forth from the deserted shower stalls to the expanse of dirt road that divided a thick forest area. There were more marines milling about, so she kept her head down and no one noticed her. She couldn't face them. It was too soon. She was on the verge of tears. It happened every time after leaving a field hospital. Seeing smiles on those broken men—their bravery— hiding her sadness. It broke her.

Patty walked past the mess tent. It was much quieter now. The smell of turkey overpowered the coffee aroma.

Veering off the road into the woods, she reached the clotheslines. There were fewer clothes on the lines, making room for the shirt and pants that she slung over one of them. The card game was still going on when she placed the helmet next to the firepit and headed out.

She didn't get far. That red mini-dress was like a beacon in a fog.

"It was a great show." A marine stepped in time beside her.

"Thanks."

"You look nice."

"Thanks." Patty kept moving.

She could see the tent and wanted to get to it before a crowd gathered. "That's my tent," she pointed to it. "Nice talking to you."

She shook hands and noticed his surprised look at her hasty retreat. "See you later," she said, making a beeline for the tent.

As expected, Jackie wasn't there. It was too hot to be cooped in. Besides this was the time for mingling with the men. Belly-flopping on her cot, she kicked off her heels and buried her face in the pillow, muffling barely contained sobs.

She thought of Christopher and wondered what it was like for him here. He was like their mother, a kind, fun-loving person. Brutality wasn't part of his nature. She was like her dad. But this place could still break her down. She couldn't imagine what the emotional stress would do to Christopher. Even though he tried to sound upbeat in the letters, there was an odd time he slipped, hinting at a truth that she knew was tearing him apart. Did he go to the USO shows hoping to see her? She played out her usual fantasy: being on the USO tour and meeting up with him. Peter had come close to making the fantasy real. He was so much like Christopher.

She got off the cot, picked up her shorts, and shook the wrinkles out of them. Her mini-dress fell to the floor in a puddle of red as she stepped into the shorts. She smelled the armpit of the cotton sleeveless ruffled top and decided it was time for a change, so she put on a clean one. Tidying their space, she gathered strewn clothes and toiletries and shoved them into her bag hung on a nail hammered into a post in the middle of the tent.

Peter called from the zippered flap. "Patty, are you there? It's me, Peter."

"What."

"I've come to escort you to lunch."

"It's that time already?"

"We're having turkey. The cooks made it special for you girls."

"So, I heard," Patty said. "Goddamn it."

"What's wrong?"

"I tripped and hit my toe." She kicked Jackie's running shoe out of the way. "Goddamn metal leg." She sat on the cot, squeezing her big toe. After the throbbing subsided, she put her socks on.

"Anything I can do?"

"Just give me a minute," she said, tying up shoelaces. Shortly afterwards, she came out of the tent.

"You changed." Peter sounded disappointed.

"You want the mini dress? I'll get it for you. Looks like you've got nice legs."

"Better than most," he smirked hiking his pants up to his knees and modeling his calves. "We'll take the road it's easier walking. How's the foot?"

"Toe. I'll survive."

A steady stream of men came out of the barracks area and headed to the mess tent. When Patty walked into the wood-frame structure with canvas sides and roof, it was like the school bell had rung for recess. Marines, more like little boys, elbowed and shoved each other out of the way as bodies fell in line behind her. The smells of Christmas turkey and gravy wafted through the air and clung to the heavy waterproof canvas tent.

Boisterous laughter and flirtatious babble competed for attention with the cutlery that clicked against tin plates and stacked trays. She liked that Peter wasn't part of the mindless herd. But it was his lie about being her brother that assured him a place beside her. She held out her tin plate and watched as creamy blobs decorated with yellow kernel corn plopped onto it. A large scoop of mashed potatoes, three slices of turkey, and beets filled the rest of her plate. The coffee smelled surprisingly good.

There were two open picnic tables, so the men didn't know which one she would go to. With each step she took, six other legs crowded her body. The race was on when she turned in the direction of a table. Then Patty did a quick turnabout to the other table. Peter sat beside her on the bench. He grinned at the smile that lit up her face as the men scrambled to secure a spot. After some shoving, the weaker personalities were bullied away from the table, leaving the remaining men tightly packed.

"You sure know how to piss people off," Peter said.

"That's nothing, watch this." Patty reached over to the next table and tapped Jackie on the shoulder. Peter leaned back, to hear their conversation without turning around.

"What's the matter?" Patty asked Jackie.

"What do you mean?" Jackie sounded annoyed. She didn't like being interrupted when she was in the limelight.

"You're frowning so bad."

"No, I'm not."

"Oh, sorry. It's the eyebrows. It must be the heat. It looks like they've grown together."

Jackie's hand flew to her eyebrows, and she put her head down. She excused herself from the table and said she had to go to the lady's room.

"They call it the latrine," Patty said.

Jackie paid no attention as she rushed out of sight.

"I don't get it," Peter said.

"My brother Christopher would have had lots of fun teasing her. She plucks out her eyebrows and then draws them on with an eyebrow pencil. She says all the Hollywood beauties do it. It gives me so much to work with." Patty cupped a hand around her ear to block out the loud talking and noise. "I'll walk up behind her, and when she turns around, say, 'Sorry, I didn't mean to startle you,' while I raise my eyebrows. Sometimes, I don't have to say anything. I just tilt my head and stare at her eyebrows."

Peter laughed. "Does she fall for it every time?"

"It never misses. She's so obsessed with her looks; she can't take a chance that for once it won't be a joke."

Between bites of food, Peter looked over at Jackie and laughed. The turkey was delicious. Patty was surprised at how quiet the men were. Everyone concentrated on their meal. Most had eaten up in record time and were working on seconds. Playing with her beets, Patty wasn't used to eating this heavy a meal for lunch.

"If you don't want your beets, I'll have them," the marine across the table said to her. He smiled at the guy beside him and said, "I'll be peeing red tomorrow and dropping a purple-headed anaconda. It'd be a double flusher if we had toilets."

"I miss watching those swirlies," the marine beside him said. "Logs the size of your forearm, so big they stand on end and swirl around." They both laughed.

Patty had never heard this kind of conversation around a dinner table before. *My mother would have been mortified.*

"So, why did you join the USO?" Peter asked.

"I was too old for Girl Scouts."

"No, I really want to know."

She hadn't told her best friends and certainly wouldn't tell a stranger. When Christopher got drafted, he and their dad fought. Christopher threatened to go to Canada with drafted buddies. Their dad wouldn't hear of it. She came home one day to see their hands around each other's throats, but neither of them could squeeze. They were like that for a while, with equal parts of rage, before breaking apart. Since then, her dad was impossible to talk to. When she'd tried to make him see Christopher's side, he'd change the subject or go quiet. Bullied constantly, Christopher gave in and reported for duty.

Patty resented her father for doing that. Christopher should have had control over his life. He was twenty-two and not a kid who had to answer to his dad anymore.

She moved her food around her plate. "I wanted to see my brother. He's stationed at Da Nang."

"Shit, you should have settled for a picture. Sorry, that sounded bad." Peter avoided looking at her and went back to eating his lunch.

"Are you a lifer?" Patty asked, wanting to break the uncomfortable silence.

"No, they had to drag me here kicking and screaming all the way."

"My brother was the same."

"We gotta do, what we gotta do."

"You sound like my brother. It was hard for him because we were army brats."

"I don't envy you that life."

"It was fine until I was seventeen and started asking why. The army never explains itself and neither did my dad. They don't encourage thinking. You can only listen to 'just do it' so many times."

As their plates were emptied, the tent was filled with sounds and activity. Men got up with their cups, plates, and cutlery. Pots and pans banged in the kitchen. Jackie's outbursts of laughter attracted many of the men from Patty's table to surround hers. Patty was relieved. She preferred more intimate conversations. She wanted to know what being here was like for Peter.

"Ready?" Peter picked up his dishes and cutlery.

Patty did the same and tagged along after him to the big grey tubs in front of the kitchen where they deposited everything.

She noticed Peter looking at her running shoes. "Want to get away for a bit?"

"What do you mean?"

"There's a small waterfall about a mile from here. It flows into the Quang Tri River."

"But the ceasefire has been canceled."

He reminded her more and more of Christopher. This was exactly like one of the hair-brained ideas he would get. Just like with her brother, she would have to rein him in. "It's not safe."

"If it weren't safe, I wouldn't be going. I'm too short to risk anything now."

"Do you mean like in 'short-timer'?"

"Yeah. My time's almost up. I've been tracking my last hundred days on a calendar. Only got thirty-four left, so I'm not about to take any chances."

"Is the calendar of a nude woman with numbered squares the way to count down the days?"

"Yeah. Some guys get a little paranoid and want to hole up so nothing can happen. You know, Murphy's Law. They think Charlie's out to get them like they got a target on their back that says, 'last chance.'"

Peter continued. "It's hard because the shorter you get, the more you think about going back into the world and the harder it gets to concentrate. The more you worry, the worse it gets. If you don't concentrate, you're going to get nailed. And knowing makes it harder."

"So why would you risk it now?"

"Trust me, it's not a risk. The gooks try to sneak past us because they're packing light and know we have heavy artillery. Most of our time is spent on reconnaissance. We're trying to find the bastards. Excuse the language."

*Going on an adventure like this would be like being with Christopher. Even the C.O. said it was safe and he should know. Christopher would've teased me for being a killjoy.* "But we can't leave the base."

"Sure, we can."

*How many times had Christopher told me to throw caution to the wind and enjoy life?*

"Just south of us is the Rockpile. Great elevation. Our guys man an outpost there, and from that vantage point they can spot any movement. The only way in is by chopper. We're covered. They've got our back."

"Okay, if you're sure it's safe."

"I just need to make a pit stop and pick up my rifle."

# Chapter 4

Peter came out of his tent with a rifle and handed Patty a polaroid photograph.

"Thanks. When did you take it?"

"I remembered my camera near the end of your show and went to get it. When I got back you were just wrapping up, so I took this picture from behind you. I was afraid that by the time I got to the front of the stage, you'd be gone. And I was right. I couldn't find you." He handed her a plastic bag to seal it in.

"This is great." She sealed the picture inside the bag. It fit perfectly into the back pocket of her shorts. They walked straight out from Peter's tent, parallel to the road, up to the gate entrance.

"Where are you going?" the sentry asked.

"The waterfall." Peter handed him a small packet.

Patty had seen small packets of cocaine that looked like that.

The sentry smiled and patted Peter on the back. "Don't have her out too late."

Peter took the lead, and they walked single file down a well-worn path. Barely able to see through the seven-foot-tall grass, Patty stood on tip-toe and watched the feathery, golden waves bow and ripple in the breeze.

The yellow field gave way to tall trees with a mulch carpet, making walking difficult than on the hard pathway.

"Where are you from?" Patty asked.

"New York." Peter shifted his rifle adjusting the strap. "I'm surprised that an army man would let his daughter come over here."

"We don't exactly see eye to eye on things. He thinks I should be married and taking care of a husband instead of voicing my opinions. He said—" Patty tripped over a tree root hidden under the leaves. She paused to catch her breath. Animals scurried from one hiding place to another, foraging for food. "He said women are too emotional for politics or policies."

The only reaction was from the birds squawking in the trees. Her voice turned bitter as she quoted next, "'And the only reason a woman should be on the floor of the House of Representatives is to clean it.'"

Peter shrugged. "My dad's the same. It's how they were raised."

Patty was hoping for more of a reaction.

"You sound like a women's libber," Peter said, holding back a tree branch for her.

"Worse." Patty used her favorite saying. "I not only burnt my bras but all my bridges too. I'm an anti-war protestor."

Peter's grip on the branch released. The snap startled her.

"For God's sake, don't tell anyone else. Guys here are pissed off that they're here risking their lives while the Doves back home are safe and criticizing them."

"You think I can't handle myself? I grew up with boys who liked to put firecrackers in a frog's mouth and watch it explode. I know what they're capable of."

Peter's mouth was pulled slightly to one side in one of those, yeah sure, reactions that Patty was all too familiar with.

"The waterfall is up there." He pointed toward a gently slopping hill thick with brush.

They proceeded down a path between trees, avoiding roots that were squeezed out of the earth, to a sandy shoreline where a small waterfall, the height of a two-story house, crashed into a river. The aqua-green water quivered. She sat on the sand and took off her shoes and socks. Wiggling her toes into the hot white sand, she whistled when Peter rolled up his pant legs. They waded into the wide pool of glittering water. Patty felt ripples in the sandy bottom. They walked toward a fine mist with Peter thumping the rifle onto his shoulder. The water became deeper licking at the hem of her shorts. The closer they got to the waterfall, the more powerful was the spray. Patty turned and walked backwards into the torrent.

When Peter raised his voice, she faced him, shielding both eyes from the deluge of water.

"There's a cave at the base, behind the falls."

"I can see the opening." Her words were drowned out by the roar of the water.

The sound reminded her of when she lost the station on her transistor radio. Water crashed down from the ledge overhead onto them. They walked through the sheer wall of water inside to the blackness of the earth's layers. Peter turned on a flashlight. He advanced a short distance, then took out two candles from his pocket, placed them on either side of the cave wall in notched-out hollows, and lit them. A soft glow highlighted the stone walls and floor. Peter led the way with the flashlight illuminating icicle-like formations hanging from the ceiling designed by nature through thousands of years of metamorphosis. He took time shining the light around, so she could take it all in.

"Amazing." Patty peered up marveling at the sight. It resembled uneven rows of thin and fat icicles that hung from the edge of the roof of their house in winter. Except, these were iridescent blues, greens, and yellows. Their hues combined and changed as she walked around. It was like being in another dimension or some fairy-like place. The cave walls were rough with protrusions and holes. She could have spent hours here, but he prodded, nudging her elbow. "There's more to see."

They continued walking. Shining the light on the stone floor, he held up an arm to block her.

"Careful." He pointed out similar inverted icicles. She went up to the different shades stroking the rock wondering what made them luminous.

He shone the light around. "I told you it was worth the trip."

"This is incredible. How did you find it?"

"One of the guys did. Now, a lot of us come here for a shower or a swim. It beats lining up at the stalls." Peter checked his watch. "We should get going. There's even more." He led the way back to the entrance and snuffed out the two candles.

The bright sun hit them like a spotlight when they left the cave and waded to the shore where they had left their shoes. Plunking down on the ground next to their things, Peter pulled out a plastic bag from his pocket and handed it to her.

She looked at the patch of cloth inside. "What's this for?"

"To dry your feet. Get between your toes too," he instructed.

After she had used the cloth, she handed it back to him and watched while he meticulously dried each foot. He reminded her of a cousin who was obsessed with weird stuff like that.

"Feel up to climbing to the top of the hill?"

"That'd be great." She loved the exertion of a climb.

Trekking the well-worn trail scraped bare of grass and stones, they headed up the path. Patty brushed off his proffered hand. "I'm fine," she said, balancing on a large tree root protruding from the ground. The gradual incline made the climb easier than other hikes she'd been on with her father.

Closer to the top of the hill, massive, smooth bedrock protruded from the earth. Climbing up to the level ground, they came to moss-covered rocks by the river's edge. Flat partially submerged stone shelves divided the short distance from one shoreline to the opposite. Water gurgled frothing up and over three large boulders at the precipice reaching the earth's spout to pour over the edge and plunge into the gurgling belly of the river below.

"It's incredible."

Peter gave her time to take everything in—the tropical foliage, sun sparkling on the water, sounds—its power consuming. "Amazing. Isn't it?"

"I feel like I'm on top of the world." Patty spread her arms wide over her head. Because she was on flat ground, her fear of heights hadn't kicked in.

Peter looked down to adjust his rifle. "Your shoelace is undone."

When she knelt to tie it up, Peter held out his hand and waited to help her up. Finishing with the shoelace, she took his hand and smiled up at him.

The sound of metal spoons rattling against a metal sheet was confusing. She wondered if the sounds from the mess tent could travel this far when Peter's hand yanked from hers. His terrifying scream seemed never-ending. She covered both ears. His face twisted in pain while his body jerked in a bizarre dance—torn apart by rapid gunfire. Flesh and blood spewed from his chest hitting Patty in the face, splattering. She gasped for breath, tasting blood. Peter's body thrust forward almost landing on top of her. Blood streamed down her face. She thought she was screaming but no sound would emerge. Peter's eyes and mouth were open, but no breath came from him. She couldn't remember touching him. She must have. Plowing her blood-soaked hands through the grass to clean them, she wanted to run. But her legs wouldn't support her. She slumped to the ground and dragged herself back over to the slabs of stone and hid behind shrubs to catch her breath. Then she nose-dived downhill, spreading her arms out in front to control the momentum. With her knees scraped raw, she retraced the route they had taken earlier, willing her body on. With arms shaking and elbows scouring on twigs and stone shards, she crawled down the hill.

Reaching the bottom, she skirted the edge of the rock face and walked into the calm water. Wading to the back of the falls, she collapsed onto the cave floor. Laying on the hard bumpy stone, she listened to a series of loud cracks give way to explosions. The sky was filled with orange and red flames that reflected through the waterfall— like wavy streams of dripping blood.

After a time, the steady din of gunfire got closer. It was ringing inside her ears, echoing inside her mind. Inching farther back into the cave, she envisioned Peter's face and tried not to feel the pressure of his hand being torn from hers. But he was like a phantom limb. She felt his hand in hers, saw the agony on his face. Then she collapsed.

# Chapter 5

The C.O. had been busy writing up a report on the day's activities when he heard the thunk from mortar rounds leaving their tubes. The Lieutenant ran into the C.O.'s office, awaiting orders. The first round of mortars exploded inside the camp.

"Find those girls and bring them here," the C.O. barked.

Already out of his chair and crossing the tent to get to his radio, the C.O. pressed the on button.

"Four two, this is six two, over."

"Go ahead, six two, over," a voice on the other end responded.

"We're getting hit hard and we have civies. I repeat civies that need to be evaced on priority status, over."

"Roger that, six two." There was silence for a moment while he checked on the availability of a chopper and pilot.

"Six two, Wilco. Over and out."

The kitchen staff grabbed their helmets and rifles that had been stashed beside the canned goods in a far corner of the mess tent. Jackie sat dumbfounded not sure what to do. Marines ran from the table, bumping into kitchen staff who ran toward her. A helmet was slapped on her head as the rough wooden bench scraped the back of her legs when two marines pulled her off it and took her out the door. A large marine wrapped his arm around her waist, and hollered, "Keep up."

The two of them ran together, joined at the hip, while surrounded by a small army of marines with their rifles pointing outward as they ran to the C.O.'s tent. Men scattered in every direction. Some were headed to the barracks area to retrieve their rifles and helmets. Others were going to preassigned destinations to locate artillery rockets, grenade launchers, bazookas, and mortars.

Jackie arrived at the C.O.'s tent with her escorts.

"Where's the other one?" the C.O. demanded.

"No one's seen her since supper, sir." The Lieutenant yelled over the explosions.

"You must know where she is?" the C.O. asked Jackie while strapping on his gun.

"The last time I saw her, she was leaving the mess tent."

"Was she with anyone?"

"She must have been."

"She's probably with her brother," the lieutenant offered.

Examining the scratches on the backs of her legs, Jackie said, "Her brother is in Da Nang."

The Lieutenant tilted his head.

"Someone has to know where the fuck she is. Take some men," the C.O. said, "and find her."

It was a while before the lieutenant and the men returned.

The C.O. shouted, "I just heard from the pilot. He'll be here in ten. He's got thirty seconds once he lands. Get her the hell up that hill. You three," he pointed to the marines with grenade launchers and a bazooka, "cover them at the landing zone. The rest of you are escorts. Get the fuck going."

The chopper arrived and the pilot set the timer. The men hadn't found Patty. The C.O. watched as the chopper took off with Jackie on board, and was safely out of range. Bursts of orange and red exploded in all directions. It had been a long time since the base had suffered a major assault. Usually, the North Vietnamese and Viet Cong hit hard and fast and retreated. There was no sign of them retreating. Their tactics had changed.

The marines at Ca Lu battled most of the night with choppers coming and going regularly to pick up the casualties. The C.O. made sure all the wounded were out. Listening to the whistling and the familiar ear-splitting boop, boop, boop of the bombs, the marines were good at figuring out where they would land, and darted out of the way. Screaming artillery came on in streaks of light. The darkening sky was lit up with explosions and bright bursting clouds.

Claymore mines with tripwires attached to the concertina wire exploded, killing the enemy trying to infiltrate the camp. Their corpses brought down the wire and covered the sharp blades. Walking over the bodies of their comrades, the enemy entered the base. Marines screamed, "Gooks in the wire." Shouts of "Broken arrow," could be heard throughout the base in different locations when the C.O. gave the order to retreat. He had given up on trying to find Patty.

∗∗∗

Patty's shirt chilled her body as she slept on the cold weathered stone. Sucking up the stench of mold and mildew from the shale floor, she sat up and thrust her body upward. Her hands pushed, fingers squishing into the furry slime that clung to the stones. She wasn't sure whether she had fallen asleep or fainted.

Fear gripped her heart, tearing at her insides. Sitting on the cold slab, enclosed in dull grey stone, she reached into the darkness, stretching into the endless void. The blackness of the cave triggered childhood fears of monsters and demons that lurked in every corner.

Grazing her knees on the rough stone, she crawled, feeling trapped in the jaws that had swallowed her whole. Eyes open but unseeing, she made her way through the eerie cavity and touched, what she imagined was, a giant tooth, using it to prop herself up. She walked as if being pulled, arching her spine, and stretching out her hands to detect what she couldn't see.

Assuming she was heeding the noise of the waterfall and not its echo, she was reassured when she saw a shaft of light. Slowly, she headed for the entrance and the thunderous noise of the water. Patty peered through the heavy curtain of drizzle towards the hillside. There was no one in sight.

Her fingers ran through tangled hair, but they caught in dried blood. Looking down at her sleeveless top, she saw pieces of raw flesh and blood, pieces of Peter that had splattered and dried on the paisley print. She cupped her hand around her mouth and felt crusty lumps of flesh that were stuck to her cheek. Her body shuddered as the macabre scene raced through her mind.

She remembered Peter's smile that had turned into a gaping black hole when he screamed. The shock on his face and the holes that were blown through him. Struggling to catch her breath, she cried in quick short pants. Her tongue, like a dry unbuttered piece of toast, scraped at the roof of her mouth. Bile threatened to rise and choke her as she walked into the center of the falls where the water cascaded down on her.

Struggling for breath, she let the force hit her to wash her hair and clothes. The pounding shower forced her to step out from underneath periodically to draw gulps of air. She cried. The reality hit her as hard as the water. Poking her head out from the falls, she saw thick purple smoke clouds in the direction of Ca Lu. The smell of sulfur clogged her nose, burned her eyes, and made them water. Everything was quiet.

She thought of Peter. *He should have been going home. It wasn't fair. Why did we come here? Why couldn't we have stayed at the camp? Someone must be looking for us. Maybe I should stay here until they come. Maybe they forgot about me. Maybe they're too busy with the wounded. What if no one comes?*

Stepping from the mouth of the cave, Patty walked out from under the waterfall. Fog or maybe smoke hung over the ground. It gave her a sense of relief that she couldn't be seen but also fear of walking into the unknown. Keeping close to the base of the hill, she watched for anyone coming her way and waded to the water's edge.

She sat on the sandy shoreline and dumped the water out of her shoes. Bird-dogging the shoreline, the soles of her shoes flicked up sand. She climbed up the path, stepping over tree roots and boulders, putting one foot in front of the other.

Concentrating on the climb was all Patty would allow herself to think about. Periodically she checked her bearings. The noise she made treading through the bush seemed exaggerated compared to the quiet. Silence replaced the bird and animal sounds she had heard earlier. The fog was lifting. She recognized a group of overturned trees and headed in that direction. It brought her out to the path with the yellow willowy field. The sun was starting to dry her clothes. Her eyes darted in every direction, scanning the area to ensure the enemy was not lurking about.

When she came within a few yards of the camp, she ran. Smoldering embers were all that was left of the army village. Death hovered over the land like a shroud over a mass grave. Blood splattered the earth like rain leaving puddles too numerous for even the ground to absorb. Mangled, dismembered bodies lay strewn in twisted heaps, eyes wide from shock, lips contorted. The stench of blood and excrement assaulted her senses. Her head reeled in protest. Doubling over, she slumped to the ground clutching her stomach in heaving spasms.

She was seeing up close what she had protested at home. *What are we fighting for? Everyone's dying and no one knows why. So many.* Ragged puffs groaned from her chest. *How many?* Tucked into the fetal position, she rocked back and forth. What at first seemed like a calming technique now turned into a forceful, measured rhythm that consumed her.

"How many?" she accused. Her whisper invaded the silence. Surrounded by corpses, her sing-song chant matched her rhythm.

"Hey, hey L.B.J. how many kids did you kill today? Hey, hey L.B.J. how many kids did you kill today?" In her mind, she was back at Capitol Hill protesting.

\*\*\*

Patty's voice had become hoarse, and her legs were cramped from sitting cross-legged for so long. But every time the cameras rolled, new energy had been found to shout the chant that sent fists hammering out the beat. "Hey, hey L.B.J. how many kids did you kill today?"

The police had cordoned off Capitol Hill, keeping spectators, reporters, and camera crews behind the boundary. The line had been drawn. College kids wearing blue jeans, tie-dyed T-shirts, headbands, and love beads held up signs of protest and offered sage advice: "Make love, not war."

The protestors heckled and taunted the police who had formed a human wall, shoulder to shoulder, shield touching shield, visors down, and ready for action. They had been the only force that stood between anarchy and Capitol Hill. The politicians had thought better of bringing in the army, but had kept them on alert. It was a circus-type atmosphere with protest songs about war, sad songs about death, and poems that echoed through megaphones.

Huddled bodies trapped curling smoke and sucked up the skunk smell of a freshly lit joint. An old slug bug, a hand-painted Volkswagen Beetle, with a peace sign emblazoned on the front, backfired. She thought it had been a gunshot. She remembered the fear—feeling they were being fired on and that she was about to die.

It was that same feeling that made her react to what was happening now. Fear forced her out of her thoughts and brought her back to lie among the dead in Ca Lu.

Patty uncurled her body and stood shielding her eyes to limit her view. She walked through piles of charred wood and debris. Lying out in the open was a severed hand. There was no body. The fingers were curled up except for the index finger which was pointing—Peter Pointer. Her eyes stared while disjointed thoughts pockmarked her reality. Peter Pointer, pieces of Peter. *Peter Pointer picked a peck of pickled pieces.* She couldn't take her eyes off the severed hand. Patty's high-pitched laugh was uncontrollable as she pointed her finger, imitating the hand on the ground. "Uncle Sam wants you and you and you. Join now before it's too late."

She pointed to each of the bodies, then stopped. She couldn't tell if this bunch of body parts was one or two or several men. Making a breathless choking sound, sickened by her laughter and the smell of death, she sucked on her bottom lip, forcing back a wail of hysterical giggles. She was disgusted by her ghoulish reaction but unable to control it.

She had to get out of there, but needed supplies. Shielding her eyes with her head down, she maneuvered around the corpses. Walking towards the mess tent, she stopped at what had been the kitchen. A dead soldier lay on the ground with a helmet next to his dark thick brush-cut head that looked more like a toupee on his white scalp. She picked up the helmet. The words "Born to Breed" were written on it in a wide black magic marker. Disgusted by the words, she dropped the helmet. Buried in explosions of C-rations, an M16 was pinned underneath him, hidden. Her fingers touched bubbly pockets of flesh when she rolled him over. The thud of his hand slapping the ground was startling. She grabbed his rifle. Unbuckling the belt, and tugging on it, she freed it from around his waist. The belt contained clips of ammo and a Colt .45 caliber pistol that sat in a leather pouch.

She strapped the belt around her hips and positioned the M16 across her back. Digging through the rubble, she spied another helmet with no writing on it. Tucked inside the helmet was a picture of a girl and an Ace of Spades. Picking up a rucksack, she dumped out its contents. She felt bad about tossing the letters and photographs inside—throwing away the owner's life like it didn't matter. Shaking two canteens of water, she figured they were full. She discarded the shovel, but kept the water, machete, a pair of clean socks, shirt, jacket, and rain poncho, stuffing them back into the rucksack. She was surprised to find an overlooked hand grenade when it rolled out from between the layers of the poncho. Although Patty knew how to fire an M79 grenade launcher, her father would never allow her to handle a hand grenade, so she wasn't about to now.

The ground was littered with boxes of C-rations from collapsed shelving. Each box contained twelve meals with many tin cans. Their lids were stamped with their content and included dinners, fruits, desserts, candy, crackers/bread, and cheese. Patty sorted through the cans picking out her favorites. Even though she wasn't a fan of ham with lima beans or beans W/Frankfurter chunks in tomato sauce, she thought they would taste better than the others without being cooked. She also took fruit, pound cakes, cheese and crackers, peanut butter, jams, desserts, chocolate bars, and candy. A lot of items, but many of them were in small containers. It shouldn't take that many days to find the base, but as her dad always told her, be prepared, and expect the worse. With the amount of food she had, she was packed for a long haul.

She opened the accessory pack to see if she needed anything in it. It had four can openers, cigarettes, matches, chewing gum, toilet paper, coffee, cream, sugar, salt, and a spoon. She tossed aside the coffee, condiments, and cigarettes and put everything else into the rucksack.

Patty thought about the map the C.O. had shown her. Camp Carroll was farther north and Khe Sanh was west on Route 9, he had said. So that she didn't get lost, she would stay close to the road, but stay deep in the woods. Flinging the straps of the nylon rucksack over her shoulder, she tucked her hair into the helmet and headed toward Khe Sanh.

According to her watch, three hours had passed, and she had long since lost sight of the road. She plodded over land permanently scarred, browned by chemicals, and destined to remain barren. It was like passing through a black-and-white picture with nothing defined and everything that same dead stain. Dry branches and twigs snapped under her rubber soles. No bugs or insects, no mouse or animal inhabited this dead zone, even they needed more than this land could offer.

She saw a jungle in the distance and was immediately drawn to its hues. Khe Sanh could be on the other side. Relieved to get out of the sun, she walked into the thicket's shade. Leaves from massive trees acted like umbrellas. Dull brown shades were replaced by purple elephant grass, and fluted-shaped orange flowers edged in yellow popped up from a carpet of green leaves. The jungle would offer more protection she assumed.

The leather on her wristwatch was sweaty and tighter. Patty had no idea how far she had gone or where she was. Her arms and legs stung from the elephant grass's razor-sharp serrated edges. Vines and mahogany trees, thick with leaves, made the jungle feel like a huge living maze. Patty felt the weight of her rucksack pulling on her shoulders. Broad leaves slapped at her face as she tried to clear a path. She stopped swatting flies and insects because, as quickly as she whooshed them away, they were back again in a steady swarm.

Grabbing at a branch that was in her way, she cried out in pain. A large, purple-colored thorn had embedded itself into the palm of her hand. She pinched the visible part of the thorn between her thumb and index finger and yanked it out. The thorn came out with bloodied pink flesh dangling from its curved spearhead.

She wanted to cry but pictured her father saying, "It's a long way from your heart, so spit on it and go back out and play." Debating about washing the wound, she decided not to waste the water. Cutting a strip off the bottom of the clean shirt in the rucksack, she wrapped her hand with it.

Bushy trees with long branches hanging, tangled masses of thorny vines surrounding her. She re-adjusted the M16 so the weight from the rucksack held it in place. Flattening herself out, belly to the ground, she dragged herself with her head low to avoid the stabbing thorns. Elbows and knees rocked from side to side as she inched ahead until exhaustion overwhelmed her. She lay there, watching day turn to night.

Disturbed by her shifting weight, insects buzzed from one sore muscle to another. Licking her lips, she tasted dew dripping from leaves. During the night, her long hair spilled out of the helmet and got tangled in an overhead branch. As she worked to separate the clump of hair, thorns repeatedly pricked her hands. Using a knife, she hacked the hair free.

She crawled once more. Whenever she was careless to overstep boundaries, the thorns were quick to punish. With each exertion, her nostrils flared and sucked in the dampness. Pushing her body along without slowing the pace, she didn't stop crying or crawling. One seemed to aid the other. She plucked a large broad leaf from a plant in front of her and used it to wipe her eyes and blow her nose. Periodically, she dropped her head onto the soft cushion of her arm, disturbing insects.

Closing her eyes, wanting to forget this torture, she crept on, imagining these movements to be part of a choreographed dance. She pictured the theatre. It was another night with only a few vacant seats. She swirled onto the stage in perfect synchronization. With arms extended and feet moving simultaneously, she kept a steady fluid pace. The rough ground and exposed tree roots scratched at her, a reminder of the reality she was trying to forget.

Whether dancing or singing, it was always another bit part, with a lousy paycheck, which meant another morning working at the diner serving greasy bacon and eggs. When her arm brushed a branch, she was surprised that there were no consequences for the action. She opened her eyes and saw a patch of blue sky. The thorny bushes had disappeared, but the jungle was still dense.

Rising and walking to a large rock, she sat on it and yanked leaves off an overhanging tree branch. She splashed water over her mouth and wiped the dirt off before taking tiny sips of water. Using large leaves as towels, she rubbed her legs and arms taking off layers of dirt and spots of blood. She looked at the dirty bandage on her hand. *Why didn't I get a first-aid kit?* She had been close to the infirmary. She thought of the men: the Italian stud, Miles, the young boy, and the others, and expected the C.O. had gotten them out. *If only I'd said no to Peter maybe, he'd be alive, and I'd be in Saigon eating rice and fish.*

It had been a while since she last ate. Patty opened her rucksack and picked up the tin can of ham and lima beans. The can opener looked like a small metal letter "r" with P38 on it. Stabbing the pointy end into the edge of the can, it let out a whooshing sound as the pressure seal broke. She pumped the opener around the can. It was hard to do, and it kept getting stuck, so she had to restart it. Almost everything was in a tin can. A lot of work. *This better be good.* She unwrapped the cellophane from the spoon, dipped it into the can, and took a big mouthful. Gagging, she spat it out. She couldn't imagine anyone able to swallow this putrid stuff. She opened the crackers and cheese and ate them with beans and Frankfurter chunks. Scooping a spoonful, she tested it with her tongue. It was much better. She wolfed it down. Plucking out the other two cans of Lima beans and ham from her rucksack, she discarded them in the bushes with the rest of the opened cans. At least it would lighten her load. Ripping another leaf off the tree, she wiped her hands.

Forcing herself off the rock, she picked up the rucksack and headed out. It had been moral to say that she had come here to help her brother, but it had mostly been to punish her father. Whenever she tried to talk to him, her father always had to get back to something important—something more important than her. He never asked about the dance troupe, the auditions she went to, or the bit parts she got. Never showed up at any of her performances. Not even the first one when she'd been so excited.

The only question he ever asked was, "When are you going to get a real job?" And after her dad had treated Christopher so badly, she decided to make him pay. But she had expected to be safe, tucked inside army regulations. If she was reported missing in action, her father would be devastated. She had never meant to hurt him like this.

Even though the thorny vines had disappeared, the foliage was still thick, forcing her to use the machete. The blade's weight made her hand ache from hours of cutting her way free. If she touched a vine, it constricted around a hand or arm, similar to a flicked whip, pulling her back as she walked forward. They groped her body like unwanted hands as she slashed free. Often, the wooden handle pressed into the raw flesh left by the thorn, and the cut started bleeding again. To relieve the pain that traveled from hand to arm, she periodically switched the machete to her opposite hand.

The pulsing, searing pain was constant. She didn't want to change direction in case she ended up back in the thorns. *Should have known by the quiet that this wasn't a safe place.* She hadn't seen or heard any animals scurrying about. They knew better than to be here.

Over time, the jungle changed again. Vines thinned out. Monkeys chattered in the distance. Getting clear of the vines, Patty sat under a large tree and tried to put the machete down. She couldn't open her hand. Her fingers had stiffened around the handle. She had to pry her fingers open to release the implement.

Her hand burned and tingled. Blood had dried around the knot in the bandage making it difficult to undo. When the material ultimately gave way, she cleaned the cut sparingly with water. Cutting another piece from the clean shirt in the rucksack, she replaced the old bandage with a fresh one.

Her hand wouldn't close tight enough to hold the small can opener. Flexing fingers and hands to get them working again made it easier to grip. She managed to open a can of spaghetti and meatballs.

Sunlight barely squeezed through trees, as ominous grey dusk descended upon the green leaves. She was surrounded by dark scurrying movement. She laid the M16 beside her on the ground. Knowing how cold it could get at night, and needing an additional layer to combat the mosquitos and varmints, Patty put on the jacket. Unrolling the rain poncho, she laid out the rubber outer shell, then put the thick liner encased by a polyester batting on top, and nestled between the layers.

The pistol jammed into her side when she rolled over. Afraid the safety might come off during the night, she unbuckled the belt and laid it within easy reach, spotting a centipede. Its length was from arm to fingertip. Using the butt of the M16, she beat it to death. Crawling back into the poncho, she tied the grommets attaching the rubber to the liner. Grateful it would protect her, she fell into an exhausted sleep.

# Chapter 6

She was thankful, she'd packed so much food when days turned into nights and the weather changed from sun to rain. When it rained, she took cover and stayed put until it stopped. The rain turned the ground to mud and made it difficult to walk. She hadn't counted on these delays. A squawking noise sounded like something from Alfred Hitchcock's "The Birds." Patty covered her head expecting to see hundreds of feathered creatures swooping down but was surprised to see only a few. White streaks of light glared through the haze of dawn. Unfolding her stiff legs, she stretched the muscles down to her toes.

She rolled over and reached for the M16. The cold steel with the power to knock her off balance reawakened childhood memories. The rifle reminded her of good times with her father at the firing range. The general enjoyed her progress and bragged about how good she was. She wanted to please him. He was respected and revered. Just walking with him made her feel important. She was Daddy's little sharpshooter. Over the years, she handled everything from pistols to automatic weapons and medium artillery. Her father taught her not only how to fire weapons, but how to clean them and take them apart. He said shooting was more than just pulling a trigger.

Like a tap turned off, adolescence had ended it all. At seventeen, her opinions and views on life were too much for him. He started taking her brother instead. Christopher hated going, but their father dragged him there anyway. "Do you want to be beaten by a girl?" Her father berated Christopher often and nicknamed him "Bullsass," teasing that he couldn't hit the broadside of a barn. The general called her "Bullseye."

Patty stood and shook her legs to relax them. A dancer's life of strict routine had made morning exercises a part of waking up, like yawning or rubbing her eyes. Warming and stretching her muscles were important now, considering the rigorous day ahead. After bending her back and touching her hands to the ground, she raised her torso.

Then, she saw it. A buffalo. Its large eyes stared at her, and its massive muscles flexed as it shifted bulk, grunting a low rumbling sound. She knew these animals were domesticated. She'd seen kids riding on their backs. But she'd heard of wild ones too. She was afraid of moving lest it charge.

The rifle was on her right side next to the tree trunk. It would take only two steps to get it. The buffalo's nose twitched, snorting up her fear, and advanced. Its hooves trampled twigs and branches, instantly turning them into mulch. She leaped for the weapon but tripped on a surface root. She might as well have been signaling to it the way her arms flew up and out in every direction before falling to the ground. Grabbing the M16, she jumped up to face the beast.

The rifle had never seemed heavier. With her hands shaking, she couldn't control her aim.

The beast bolted toward her. Its speed surprised her. She took several deep breaths and imagined herself looking at a paper target. A calm self-confidence steadied her aim to align perfectly with the prey. She pushed the selector lever to the semi-position taking off the safety. Her feet were planted, ready for the recoil, but her finger froze on the trigger.

A noise from the tree above distracted her. It happened quickly. High up, branches flew apart and leaves fell off as a basket careened through the air. She couldn't take her eyes off it. She couldn't concentrate on the buffalo either when the tree had just unleashed another danger. A massive mud ball shot from the basket. Taking her finger off the trigger, Patty leaped behind a tree as the ball broke apart releasing numerous bamboo stakes.

Hissing deadly blades sliced through stagnant air penetrating the buffalo's hide. The animal let out horrible squeals before falling to the ground. It went silent and didn't move. She waited and watched, but nothing happened. She walked to where the animal lay. Its thick hide looked like an oversized pincushion, with blood seeping from every opening.

Then she saw the clue to the mystery. Wrapped around the buffalo's cloven hoof was a trip wire which must have activated the monstrous slingshot. It wasn't long before flies and insects clustered around the bloody spears and buried themselves in the raw flesh. *That could have been me.*

Weak-kneed, she gathered her belongings before other animals smelled the feast. She picked up a stick, using it like a blind person would a cane, and fanned it out in front of her, checking for trip wires. She kept a vigilant pace, wary of unforeseen dangers. The heat intensified as the day wore on.

Her new adversary was the jungle. She could be lost for days in this maze, trapped without food or water. Perspiration trickled down her legs. Her body was dotted, splashed by mud from the increasing number of puddles. Trampled vines made her think she was on a footpath that had been cut over time. Although the path made walking easier, she was afraid of running into the enemy and veered off into the bush.

Branches scratched her, and droplets of blood appeared and attracted mosquitoes that stuck to her sweat. The density of trees was thinning, allowing her to see that the sun had shifted. The openness of the bright blue sky was a relief from the dark, claustrophobic jungle.

In the distance, she saw a flooded field. Elephant grass circled submerged rice paddies. She walked toward the fields. She'd seen

Vietnamese farmers using sickles to cut rice stalks, making bundles, and tying them together. They hauled their harvest at either end of a wide plank balanced on their shoulders. Marines called it an idiot stick. If she harvested some rice, she could add the grains to her C-rations to make the food go further, and taste better. She thought maybe they would soften up if they were soaked in the sauce from the beans and Frankfurters, or from the stew gravy. But what did she know? She wasn't much of a cook. Sandwiches were her thing.

Tall straight thick blades of grass housed golden-brown stalks. Rice sprouted from stalks that bowed from the weight, strung like pearls on a necklace. Her feet sunk deep into mud that was topped by four or five inches of water. Scooping up a handful of stalks, she cut them off near the bottom and placed them on top of the other uncut crop. She gathered enough and tied them together and was putting them in the rucksack when voices in the distance startled her. Ducking out of sight, she sank into the muddy water, concealed by bushes and elephant grass.

The sing-song pitch of voices became louder, closer. Patty lay hidden on the watery ground watching tall grass flatten, exposing black rubber X's across the tops of dirty feet. She recognized those sandals. Marines called them Ho Chi Minh Road Sticks. They were made from old truck tires.

Not daring to tilt her head to see their faces, she sank lower until the water covered her mouth. She felt a sharp bite. A ribbon of red floated around her face. The calf of her leg was burning and itching. Another bite on her left shoulder. It felt like coarse sandpaper grinding against sensitive skin.

She turned her head, lifted her shirt, and stared into a pair of eyes on top of its reddish-black, worm-like body. A leech clung to her bare skin, digging at a tiny cut, sending rippling waves of pressure through its rubber-like body, forcing itself into the broken skin. She thought of all those tiny cuts that covered her body from the serrated-edged elephant grass. Her eyes and fist squeezed tight when she felt another pinch on her thigh. The stinging pain was unbearable.

She watched the sandals.

*Go. Please go. Just leave.* To stop herself from screaming, she clenched teeth until her jaw and temples ached. She couldn't move and wouldn't splash to attract attention. A kneading pressure pulsed with a sucking motion in her thigh. She wanted to run screaming out of the water. *How much longer?* She couldn't take it.

The voices grew excitable talking over each other, interrupting. Tears streamed down her cheeks. Grasping her shoulder, she pinched the skin but couldn't force the leech out. Blood seeped between her fingers. The pressure released another stream of blood that floated on the water painting her lips red.

She *had* to wait. Wait until those feet moved. The voices became more agitated and shriller. *Why wouldn't they leave? Go, go, her mind willed them to move.* Finally, the voices were quiet; like they had reached a decision, and their feet moved. *Not yet. Wait. Just a little longer. It's going to be alright.* The swish of their machetes receded.

Patty wanted to propel her body out of the muck, hysterically screaming, but instead, without causing more than a ripple, she eased herself from the mire. She tried to pull the leaches off. They were embedded into her flesh.

Using a knife, she dug up the pulsing rubber bodies bloated with her blood. She threw the leeches as far away as possible. Blood dripped from the open wounds running down her body. Folding cut pieces from the clean shirt, she pressed them into the wounds. In no time, the material was saturated and had to be replaced several times. It was a while before Patty had the strength to move.

Soaked, she dried her shoes as best as she could with the thick liner of her poncho and replaced the soggy socks with dry ones. It wasn't until she realized that a rice paddy meant there was a village nearby, and an enemy to harvest the crop, that she made an effort to get away.

Trudging along, elephant grass and shrubs slowly disappeared and were replaced by mahogany trees. She stopped and thought about the buffalo, then picked up a stick and entered the woods. With fewer trees, she felt reassured that it would be easier to stay clear of tripwires.

She had covered a lot of ground and was hopeful of reaching the camp. As long as she hadn't been walking in circles. The farther she walked, the denser the forest became, slowing her down again. Stiff and sore from being hunched over the stick for so long, she was caught off guard when the stick dropped into nothingness.

She teetered off-balance and threatened to fall like the stick into the void before being able to stop her forward momentum. With both feet steadied, Patty looked overhead for a basket, then below for a trip wire. There was nothing.

She dropped to hands and knees, and cleared the leaves away, then leaned back, resting her buttocks on both heels. It had been close. Below her was a pre-made grave lined with razor-sharp bamboo stakes. Her hand flew up to cover her mouth. She wondered how long her luck would hold out. Peter had voiced that same fear just before he died.

*How many more traps?* She picked up another stick and used it to scavenge the earth. Confident its weight wasn't enough to trigger another trip wire or send her into a grave, she moved cautiously through the woods. After a couple of hours, her arms ached from digging up stones and plowing up roots. The exertion slowed her progress. There were times when she wielded the stick like a weapon, beating the ground. Dusk fell over the trees while she searched for cover.

So intent had she been with head down, that when she finally looked up, tall figures lined the grey sky. She crouched under a tree. The Vietnamese weren't this tall, and it wasn't an illusion cast by the moon. For the first time in days, she felt hope. She was too far away to tell if they were American. She had to get close enough to hear them speak.

# Chapter 7

S ometimes it's the simple questions that are the hardest to answer. I hate that question, "So, how did you two meet?" Who knew then, he'd be the love of my life? We didn't get off to a good start. Then after getting to know him, I thought he was a controlling jerk, but somehow, I was still attracted to him. Danger heightened every sense, including sexual desire. Maybe it's survival. The animal instincts kick in. Who knows?

He wasn't even my type. I liked the pretty boys back then. He was caring. I saw that in him and liked it. I miss his touch. Aged with tenderness. Not like the wild passion of our first time. Okay, if I were being truthful, I'd say it was lust.

In Vietnam, we didn't act on our emotions, so everything was pent up. That's not good. A volcano waiting to erupt. Simmering to the boiling point. An explosion, when it happens—you know what I mean. It was at the Royal York Hotel in Toronto Canada. We had fled our country and just arrived. I'll never forget the scent of soap and shampoo. We went from bedding down in the dirt and squatting in the grass using leaves to a luxury room with a queen-sized bed and a posh bathroom with gold-plated fixtures.

I was the one who initiated it with a kiss. Then his large, calloused hands caressed my collarbone under a heavy winter sweater. They worked their way up to my neck and cheeks and through my hair to bring my face to meet his. Through the years, he always kept those moves. It made me feel connected to him. He recognized me before the pleasure.

His mouth captured mine—tender craving, then aggressive. He hadn't expected my response to match his lust. Seductive nibbles crawled down my neck. In one quick movement, he undid the clasp of my bra and pulled it and my sweater off together. His tongue flicked my nipples. Me arching my spine wanting more. Scooping up my buttocks, he kissed around my belly button. Oh, how my legs trembled from the thrill of it all. Every part of me tingled, needing more. Teasing me with his tongue. Gracious, I'm all in a sweat at the memory.

I stripped off his shirt and flinched when my fingertips felt wide, jagged scars that cross-hatched his back.

"It's alright," he said. "They're part of who I am."

I touched his back again showing him I wasn't repulsed and felt the strength and courage that they represented. Our clothes were strewn all over. His body slid on top of mine. The feeling, the fear came back with his weight. He sensed it was too soon after what had happened. My body stiffened like I was bracing myself.

Soko told me sex had never been that complicated before. He had been used to wham-bam-thank-you-mam with no-strings-attached relationships. Said, he felt an intimacy with me that he'd never known before. He shifted his weight off and leaned on his side massaging the lines above my nose to take the wrinkles out.

I still remember his words. "I knew I loved you when I saw you dangling from that rope. I knew it wasn't just lust." As he spoke, his penis twitched against my leg. He cupped my cheeks with his hands, the way he always did when he wanted to tell me something important, and whispered, "I'll never do anything to hurt you."

So, of course, I pulled him back on top of me and the rest is history. He wanted to pleasure me. And oh, how he did.

\*\*\*

Patty kept low to the ground as she crept toward them. Even if they were American, they could still shoot her. Many died from friendly fire. With only a few yards separating them, she squatted behind a tree to listen. Impatience with the incoherent mumbling gave her the nerve to peek around the tree. But the only sound she heard was the snap of a twig behind her.

A dull pain shot across her back as she was brutally knocked to the ground. A heavy boot crashed down and pushed her face into the dirt. She gulped for air snorting up dust. Her body shook. Fighting to quell her fear, she brought her breathing back to a regular rhythm.

Further words were smothered by the boot's pressure. Just as her thoughts were becoming disjointed, the boot lifted. A hand grabbed the back of her shirt. Fingers slipped around the elastic band of her bra and yanked her off the ground. The snap of the elastic stung her back when the captor let go after slamming her butt onto the ground. Knocking the helmet off, he exposed her long, auburn hair. She watched the helmet roll on the ground.

Taking the M16 off her shoulder, he said, "What the fuck are you doing here?"

The relief was so great that she couldn't speak and cried.

"Are you a nurse?" he asked.

She had no air for the sounds of syllables and was only able to grunt shaking her head from side to side. Tears streamed down her face.

"For Christ's sake." He handed her a broad leaf. "Blow your nose."

It took two leaves to clear both sinuses and stop her body from shaking.

He looked up when two other men approached them.

"Tarnation," one man said to the other. "Dadgum middle a-nowhere and he comes up with a white woman. Leave it to Soko."

"Back to camp," the second newcomer, a handsome blonde-haired man ordered.

Soko thwacked the helmet on her head and helped her up. Patty walked surrounded by the men, with Soko in the lead. When they were close to the camp, he stopped, held up his hand, and gave a shrill bird call before proceeding. Patty jumped, startled by a pair of eyes that appeared from under a mound of vegetation.

When they strode into camp, the group attracted a lot of attention. The handsome blonde-haired guy pulled Soko aside. They talked quietly, then Soko led her to where a rain poncho had been spread on the ground next to a freshly dug hole. He motioned her to sit on the poncho. "I'll be back," he said, then left.

She watched as he crossed the camp to join a huddled group of men. She counted nine of them. There was a lone figure off to the side cleaning his weapons. He didn't seem to pay attention to the others. The circle of men spoke in hushed tones, but she knew they were talking about her from the number of times they looked in her direction. The loner appeared to be excluded from their circle.

Soko shook his head. "Biggest offensive ever waged, and she just wandered through it. What are the odds, eh, Henry?" He smiled at the man closest to him in the circle.

"What are you going to do with her?" Henry stuffed a handful of dried fruit and nuts into his mouth and looked at one of the other men in the group. "Got any ideas, David?"

"We got a sayin—"

"You always have a saying." Soko gave him a friendly push.

"'If y'all can't run with the big dogs then stay under the porch.'"

"We're not babysitters." Henry reached into the bag for another handful.

"I'll take care of it." The blonde-haired handsome guy looked at Soko. "Find out what you can."

"Will do, Captain," Soko said.

Patty watched as Soko stood and walked in her direction. Plopping down on the liner next to her, he asked, "Hungry?"

"Yeah."

He reached into his pack and pulled out two foil packets and placed them on the liner. "Mac and cheese or chicken stew?"

"Stew, please. I feel like a Saint Bernard," she said, feeling at the corner of her mouth for drool.

Soko gathered a few stones and laid them in a V formation.

"I'm Patty. Soko's a strange name. Sounds Japanese."

"It's short for Sokoloski. I'm Polish." He took the liner out of his helmet, wiped it with a leaf, and set it upside down on the stones.

His square jawline and angular plain features gave him an ordinary look—*nothing to write home about*. But his body was exceptional. That V-shaped torso hinted at muscles and abbs of steel. He had a quiet confidence when he had taken over the lead back to camp. She reached into her pack and took out a handful of rice stalks.

"I've got this," she said.

"Have you eaten any?"

"No."

"Good. Raw rice will make you sick. Could even kill you."

Along with the main course, Soko dug into his rucksack and dumped foil packets of tootsie rolls, cookies, candy-coated gum, coffee, packets of sugar, creamer, salt, and a plastic spoon onto the poncho.

She watched as he poured water into his helmet. Circling his hand over the helmet he broke off chunks from a brown block the size of a bar of soap and said, "A little C-4 and a pinch of salt, and presto." When the liquid started to bubble, he opened the packet and poured it in.

"How did you do that?" Patty felt the heat around the stones.

He showed her the brown bar. "C-4—plastic explosive. It ignites the stones. It's a fire that doesn't smoke or smell. It doesn't exist but keeps on burning. How did you get here?" Soko continued stirring.

"I'm a USO entertainer." She tried not to think about the helmet sitting on his dirty oily hair. Rooting through the rucksack, she got an accessory pack and took out a plastic spoon.

"I was at Ca Lu entertaining the troops. Afterward, I was away from the camp when it got attacked. When I got back, they were all dead. I was headed to Khe Sanh. How far is it?"

"Not far enough. Lucky for you, you have a bad sense of direction."

She watched as the dried food plumped up to its original size, the liquid thickening like gravy. "What do you mean?"

"It's better not to know."

Soko placed the helmet in front of her on the poncho's liner. "Wait a minute for it to cool down." He tested the side of the helmet before handing it to her.

"Mmmm. Cooked food instead of congealed crap. And so much better than ham and lima beans."

"Nothing's worse than ham and motherfuckers."

With her head down, almost in the helmet, she hadn't come up for air.

"You'd make sparks fly from a knife and fork," he laughed.

She handed him back the helmet. When she reached for gum, he said, "Save it for when you're walking. Chewing keeps saliva in your mouth, so it doesn't get dried out."

She took the cookie instead. "Who's in charge?"

Soko pointed to the handsome guy. "The captain," he said, wiping out the helmet with a large leaf.

The men stopped talking when she walked their way and sat down beside the captain. Many of them got up and left. The captain looked about the same age as Soko, mid-twenties. Old for this war. The men's crossed arms and hostile stares made Patty feel like an unwanted intruder.

"Where are we going?" she asked.

"We're on recon," the captain said. "So, you can't come."

"I don't want to. It's too dangerous. I need a chopper to pick me up."

"Not going to happen."

"But choppers are always flying around picking up men and dropping off supplies."

Patty looked around at the few remaining men. Some didn't raise their heads. Others were drawing in the dirt as a distraction.

Henry met her glare. "Stop looking at us like we're responsible for you. Like that damsel in distress thing. Laying a guilt trip on us."

"My father's …."

"I don't care if you're Lyndon Johnson's daughter," the captain said. "You can't come with us."

Henry leaned over and whispered into the captain's ear. They both laughed.

Patty gave an exaggerated sigh. "You won't even know I'm here."

"Women," the word was a long drawl. "Jist like a hen peckin at the ground, not listenin' but all cluck."

"Shut the hell up, David."

Patty hadn't noticed Soko standing behind her.

"Why won't you radio for a chopper?"

"Because I can't." The captain motioned for the men to clear out. Everyone except Soko left.

"Yes, you can."

"I don't have a radio."

One eyebrow was raised higher than the other. *They were on recon without a radio! A radio was their lifeline. It'd be like going into battle without a weapon.* "Why don't you have a radio?"

"Radio guys are always the first to get wasted. It's the long antenna. Makes them a target. Easy to pinpoint their position. Unfortunately, the equipment got destroyed."

"Then how are you getting me out?"

"I'm not."

"Then I'm staying with you."

"You can't come with us. You'll slow us down."

"I won't have trouble keeping up."

The captain's finger bent back the thumb on his opposite hand as he spoke. "Physically, you won't be able to do what we do." His finger bent the next finger. "I can't risk the lives of all these men for the sake of one." His fingers folded back into his hand. "There are more lives at stake than you can imagine."

Patty stared at him, unable to believe what she had heard. He was like a robot ticking off the reasons why she had to die. "You can't leave me." Her shaky voice had a pleading quality to it. The captain stood up and walked away.

"You son of. . ." Her words were muffled by Soko's hand. She felt the heat from her breath trapped in his palm. With his other hand, he tightened his grip when she thrashed out her anger on his arm.

"Settle down. The captain has no choice. He has to do what's best for all, including you. He'll make sure you have plenty of food, water, and a compass with directions to the nearest camp. That's all he can do."

When he felt her body collapse and give up the fight, he pulled her up and walked her back to the rain poncho. She dropped onto the soft cushion of its double-layer quilted nylon. No one wanted to face her—least of all the captain.

"Get out your rice and I'll cook it," Soko said.

She pulled the rice off the stalks while he boiled water in his helmet. Trampling sheaves, his heavy boots crushed husks and made it easier for her to peel the rice seeds. Putting the rice in her helmet, he tossed the contents into the air. The wind blew off the dried lighter husk leaving the rice in the bottom. It didn't take long to cook. He drained the water off into another canteen and then let the rice sit in his helmet to cool. Reaching for his rucksack, he searched inside and pulled out a small foldable shovel. Standing up, he opened the shovel and started to dig.

"What are you doing?"

"Digging you a foxhole."

"I'm not getting in that grave."

He stopped digging and leaned on the shovel. "It's safer. You'll be too easy to spot out in the open and give away our location."

"I'm not going to let you bury me."

"See, this shit is why we can't bring you. Look around, we all have them." He dropped the shovel and crossed his arms.

Patty stared at David in the foxhole beside them. He was almost buried with only his head poking out.

Soko followed her gaze. "You don't have to do that. That's how he feels safe. I couldn't do it either. I want to get out fast if I need to. Can't even stand tying up the grommets on my poncho."

There was something about crawling into that hole that terrified her. A harbinger of death. She rummaged through her rucksack and pulled out the rain poncho.

"Can I stay in there," she looked at his foxhole, "with you? I don't want to be alone."

Soko went over to his foxhole and dug to make it bigger. Patty filled the empty packets from dinner with the cooked rice, put them into the rucksack, wrapped the poncho around herself, and waited until Soko was done.

He widened the three-foot-deep hole and piled the dirt above it. "Okay, it's ready," he said and dropped the shovel beside them.

Patty laid her rubber poncho in the cavity, then put the soft liner on top, and crawled between the two layers. Soko did the same. She rolled on her side, away from him, to maximize the tight quarters. Stretching out behind her, he wrapped his arm around the indent of her waist and pulled her into his hard-muscled chest to stop the trembling. She stiffened when his hand touched her shoulder and moved down her arm.

Afraid she'd given him the wrong idea, she breathed deeply and pretended to be asleep. It was hard to judge the quietness of her breathing when a pulse throbbed in her ears. Nerve endings vibrated like the taut strings of a strummed instrument. Responding to her involuntary shudder, Soko pressed his hand firmly on her arm and rubbed it up and down to ease the tremors running through her.

With his other arm, he nudged her head and offered his bicep as a pillow. His knees were tucked in behind hers and his boots scooped up her rubber soles. He made a small gagging sound before clearing his throat. Patty knew her body odor was foul, and her hair stunk like a dirty, wet dog.

She'd managed to get this far, and she wasn't going to let them go on without her. Riding on the steady rhythm of her breathing, her eyelids fluttered, capturing tiny bright shards of starlight and tucking them into blackness for the night.

When she awoke, a heavy weight rested around her waist and her body was cuddled into a reassuring warmth that molded to her shape. Patty stretched her limbs, arching her spine, squirming her hips into a comfortable mass before opening her eyes to see a hairy arm flopped over her. Embarrassed that she'd initiated this, she threw his arm off her. "What do you think you're doing?"

His palms turned up in innocence. "I wasn't doing anything. You were the one with all the moves. I was just enjoying them."

"Keep your hands to yourself."

"Then stop rubbing your body against mine—creating friction." He grinned.

Typical, Patty thought. He knew the image she'd conjure up with that word "friction." She turned on the other side and faced him with knees bent at his crotch. Closing her eyes against the barely rising sun, she fell asleep again. The night had been cold but with the rising sun came the heat. In her sleep, she'd kicked off the liner.

Her eyelids flitted as she peeked at the light rising through the trees. Her shirt had popped open exposing deep cleavage. When she rolled on her stomach, she felt Soko touch the scab on the side of her thigh. He got up and left.

She watched him gather supplies. Returning with the compass and provisions he had promised, he laid out a first aid kit and rummaged through it to find a round tin of antiseptic cream and bandages. Soaked in sweat, the rubber poncho had twisted around Patty's body. She lifted her outstretched arm and examined its redness.

"We're on volcanic rock. Could be why the dirt is red." Soko said. He pointed to the scab on her thigh. "How'd you get that?"

His clothes and face were dusted with the same red. "Leeches. I cut them out."

"You don't do that. You use bug juice."

"Sorry, Emily Post doesn't cover that in her handy tips."

He snorted, which made her smile back. He handed her a plastic bottle of bug juice. "Are there any more scabs?"

"My left shoulder and calf."

"You're lucky these didn't get infected," he said, applying the cream and bandages. "You have to be gentle taking leeches off. They can regurgitate contaminants from previous victims and cause an infection." He looked at the filthy bandage around her hand. "What happened?"

"I took out a thorn."

He unwrapped the bandage. The skin around the scab was red. "The redness isn't from the rock. It's infection. Let me fix that."

He lathered the cream on and bandaged it. "You can have this." He handed her the wound cream and bandages. "It'll clear these up in no time. Change the bandages often."

He was watching her as she opened the rucksack and stuffed everything into it. Picking up his helmet and packets of food, he walked over to the stones arranged in V formation.

Patty looked around at the other men. Some were cleaning their weapons, others were eating. She spotted the captain a few steps away. Her tongue pressed hard against the roof of her mouth.

"Is this supposed to be my survival kit?" She threw a canteen of water at him. "Is this all it takes to clear your conscience?" He caught the second canteen aimed at his chest. "Does your map show me where the tripwires or staked graves are? Hey, you, David." She looked over to the foxhole beside them. "That's your name, isn't it?"

His clothes and body were covered in red dirt.

"How long do you think I'll last out there?"

He stopped rolling his poncho and looked at her. "Not long if y'all keep this up 'cause I'll do you in myself."

Even though his voice was low, the menacing tone made it seem louder. The seriousness of his no-nonsense truth made her stop.

Soko came back with cooked oatmeal in its pouch and handed it to her.

"What other booby traps are there?" Oatmeal grains flew from her mouth with her words.

"Watch for mines and don't touch the bamboo stakes in the graves. They're called punji sticks, and they're coated with poison sometimes. Oh, and watch out for a black snake with white stripes. If you get bitten, you're done in two steps."

"Snakes!" She hadn't thought about them.

Watching the men fill in their foxholes, she threw her wrapper into theirs before Soko shoveled in the last of the dirt. She walked over to where the canteens had landed and retrieved them. Everyone was getting ready to leave.

Soko walked over to her. "What's your full name?"

"Patty Fielding."

"Where do you live?"

"Washington."

"Me too. I'd like to look you up when we get back. You know, find out how you made out. You're the kind of person who'll keep me awake at night wondering what happened to you. Good luck." Soko strapped on his rucksack and walked away.

Patty wanted them to think they had left her behind, but as soon as they were out of sight, she stuffed the rest of her supplies into the rucksack and took off in their direction. Her plan was simple. Dog their trail. What were they going to do, shoot her?

# Chapter 8

The captain had the men split up into their usual teams of two with ten yards separating each team. The vigorous march over treacherous terrain kept them vigilant in their distancing, to minimize casualties if one of them triggered a booby trap. The pace was excruciating, but the men were accustomed to the ninety-pound weights strapped to their backs, and it was no longer cumbersome. The packs had become part of their bodies, like another appendage.

Those bodies were hard unrelenting machines, programmed in every way. No movement was natural—to be natural was to be relaxed. Being relaxed slowed reaction time. Every man knew if he was injured and unable to keep up, he would be left behind. They had a timeframe. Every danger, every obstacle, had been considered. Everything—except her.

The heavily wooded forest was cluttered with fallen trees and branches. Soko observed the captain's face between large, apple-green leaves that fanned wavy heat vapors from the earth. When the captain stopped, Soko caught up to him. "Something wrong?"

The captain looked over his shoulder in Patty's direction. It wasn't difficult to tell they were being followed and who the loud follower was.

Soko looked in the same direction. "Persistent, isn't she?"

"Yeah, got to fix the problem."

David came up beside them. "She's as good trackin as my dog Gorgeous."

"Give me ten and hold the men here." The captain left.

Soko shouldered his rifle. "She's a distraction that has to be dealt with."

"So, do y'all think he'll tie her up or knock her out?"

"Knowing the Captain, he'll knock her out. It's easier and faster."

\*\*\*

Beneath a top canopy, tentacle-like limbs slithered down monstrous tall trees. Their layered curlicue branches extended down to the base and slithered along the ground to curl up, and around rocks and boulders. Some trees had a large hollow center at the base that offered a perfect hiding place. Below them was another canopy layer of smaller trees and shrubs.

Afraid that she would lose the captain and the men in the thick foliage, Patty focused on their movement, forgetting about watching her back. She hadn't noticed the Viet Cong soldier stalking her. She hadn't seen the finger on the trigger of his AK-47, ready to fire when she walked into a clearing. Her long white legs stopped him.

Patty hadn't seen any other movement besides the captain and his men until she heard the crack of a brittle twig in a different location behind her. She ducked underneath large leaves, careful not to bump the shrub when unholstering the pistol. Sitting still, she thought her eyes were playing tricks. A clump of leaves seemed to be moving—an illusion, maybe from the streak of sunlight in the otherwise darkened double-canopy forest.

There was no breeze. But that clump of leaves moved. It wasn't swaying but advanced between shrubs. The closer it got, Patty realized this clump of leaves was mounted on a floppy-brimmed hat. The Americans wore black helmets. *Another follower?* She assumed this follower was hiding from her—therefore, an enemy. She watched the leafy hat turn at the sound of branches whooshing nearby.

She kept her pistol aimed at the chest of the person with the leafy hat, as it ducked between bushes and sneaked up to the other swishing boughs. Leaves rustled when both met with an explosion of grunts. Branches snapped, and leaves shuddered in a struggle of bodies. She saw the glint of a knife. Bushes that got separated by the fight revealed the captain. She was prepared, her weapon now trained on the "leafy hat's" torso, ready to fire. She had a clear shot. The knife was coming down on the captain. Patty fired.

She couldn't believe how easy it was to kill. It was him or the captain—her choice made instantaneously. She'd been trained for this and took the shot.

Within seconds, the captain jerked her hand. "Let's go."

They ran and never spoke.

At the sound of the shot, David steadied Soko. "Y'all got the vapors?"

"Did he kill her?"

"He-ell, Captain ain't that touched in the head to give away our location."

Soko waited and watched. "What happened?" he asked when the captain and Patty came up to the group.

"It's fugazi."

"Why's she here?" David asked.

The other men had gathered around the captain. "Assholes and elbows," he said.

Soko translated for her. "Move, fast."

The men jogged through bushes, over hills easier to traverse, up and down steep rises, and along rocky terrain. Like the men, Patty knew the importance of a regular breathing pattern when running. The calves of her legs ached, and each breath dried her mouth, leaving an abrasive cavity that made swallowing difficult. Running her finger and thumb along the inside of her dry lips she gathered thick mucous webs from the corners of her mouth.

When they had enough distance from the corpse, the captain stopped. She sat on the ground and leaned her back against a fallen tree trunk. Sprawling, her arms out on either side of her body, she arched her back against the log's rounded shape sucking in deep breaths.

Soko handed her a canteen. "Wet your lips first, then take tiny sips—no guzzling."

He walked to the captain who was slouched over. "So, why'd you bring her back?"

The captain sat on a nearby rock. "She killed a gook. Couldn't knock her out and leave her there."

"What now?" Soko knelt beside him, taking a sip from his canteen.

"She comes with us."

"I thought it was settled that she couldn't come."

"Shit happens."

Soko stood up. His eyebrows met in a frown. "You don't want a fuck-up?"

"She won't jeopardize the mission. I'll make sure of that."

"You made the right decision before, just stick with it."

The captain stood up. "It's my decision to make."

"Then make the right one."

They glared at each other.

Everyone, except the loner whom the guys called Shylock, stopped what they were doing to listen.

When Patty perceived the fight was about her, she got up and moved in closer.

"I know it's hard to leave her, but it's for her own good," Soko said.

The captain was mulling it over and she was afraid he would give in to Soko's demand. She pushed passed the men to confront Soko.

"Aren't you forgetting your place? If it's alright with the captain, what's your problem?"

Soko faced her. She expected to see hatred or at least anger, but she saw neither. He showed no emotion and turned away from her.

Soko took a threatening step toward the captain. "I won't have her coming with us."

"You won't! Who the fuck are you? I call the shots here."

"I want it on record that I object to bringing her."

Patty hadn't meant to create this showdown in front of the men. But she was glad for it. She knew now, even though Soko seemed nice, that he couldn't be trusted. The captain couldn't back down now. He would lose the men's respect.

Knowing that it came down to rank, she looked for the two-bar insignia on the captain's shirt that would settle the dispute. There was no insignia on his uniform or patch above his heart that read US ARMY. The shape of their uniforms with the multi-pockets was what she expected, and she hadn't thought too much of their black dye since she didn't know the colors for all the different branches. But with no insignia or patch, something wasn't right. *Why were the soldiers looking from the captain to Soko as if wondering who would win? Rank is everything. Odd for Soko to even question an order.*

"She comes with us," the captain said. As if adding an afterthought to reassure everyone, he said, "She had no problem keeping up when we were on the run."

Soko remained silent.

"Give me your rucksack." The captain yanked it from Patty. "Empty your pockets. I'll need the helmet and rifle," he said, littering the ground with the contents of her rucksack. His anger frightened her. She knew enough not to say anything and assumed he would calm down. Temper turned his handsome features ugly.

When he took the camouflage bag off the plastic canteen, she was surprised to see the words, "for water only, do not apply canteen to open flame or burner plates." It seemed strange to imprint such obvious instructions.

He poured the water from her canteen into his much larger one. His canteen wasn't in a camouflage bag and didn't have writing on it. Her rucksack and helmet were army green, but theirs were black. He tossed her canteen, helmet, shirt, jacket, C-rations, and rucksack in a pile. Those items were kept separate from the supplies Soko had given her.

"Let me see the knife." The captain held out his hand.

Patty figured he was tossing anything American. "It's Swiss," she said.

He grabbed it from her, then handed it back. She looked at the two separate piles. "Why are you doing this?" *Why get rid of everything American when we're American?*

"That's on a need-to-know basis. And you don't need to know."

Patty rolled her eyes. *So, military.* She was surprised he let her keep the .45-caliber pistol. But she wasn't going to question him.

The captain called over one of his men. "Bury these," he said and put his hand on the American-issued products. Patty and the soldier sifted through the discarded pile while the captain picked up the supplies Soko had given her and jammed them into his rucksack.

Taking the wrappers off the gum and many of the treats, Patty stuffed them into her shorts' front pockets. The soldier picked through her C-rations and took out two cans each of peaches and pound cake. His hands worked with lightning speed to open all the lids. Matching that same efficiency, he wadded a large chunk of pound cake into his mouth, then tilted the can of peaches, chomping the fruit down with the cake. Juice dribbled from his mouth. He finished it all with a loud burp.

The captain walked over to Patty and smiled. He looked smug and pleased with himself. "I'm going to nail Soko's ass for inciting a riot, disobeying orders, and whatever the hell else I want. He won't be competing against me again."

Patty wondered why he would say this to her. Was he so insecure, he needed to flaunt his power to impress her? Maybe he felt embarrassed by Soko challenging him. It was unheard of in the military. It had probably bruised his ego.

"That seems a little harsh." Patty knew how serious these charges were. Soko's career could be over.

Caressing her cheek, he said, "Soko may have had you, but you're mine now."

His words were like a hot poker, searing skin to brand her his newly acquired stock. These wild mood changes from anger to amorous sent a warning. She was shocked by his sudden possessiveness. His barely controlled rage that flipped to caresses reminded her of men who brutalized their wives and then begged for forgiveness.

As a curious child, she'd overheard late-night conversations between her father and others about the secret lives of violent soldiers that were guarded to protect the integrity of army life at the expense of beaten wives.

Left to speculate on what her role would be, the men's conversation became sexual—filled with lewd remarks and crude banter. Patty overheard one person say, "I'd tit fuck her before I'd boom boom, so I wouldn't need a pecker checker."

She'd heard enough and stomped over to where they sat. "Are you talking about me?"

"Yeah," a soldier named Henry spoke up. "You might say you're the butt of our jokes. But now that you're here..."

He stood up, lifted her shirt, and twisted it to rest underneath her breasts, turning her from side to side like a toy at the end of a rope. Patty tugged the thick twisted material trying to yank it from him. He laughed pretending it was a tug of war. The other men stopped laughing when she drew a knife, poking it into Henry's jacket.

"Do it," he said and stepped in closer to make her step backward. Everyone was quiet. "Do it," he insisted and crushed the knife handle into her palm.

She winced from the pain knowing the cut was bleeding again.

"Maybe I should leave you a little reminder."

Soko's larger hand moved in to cover Henry's.

Soko's demeanor wasn't threatening but amiable. He didn't say anything, just smiled and stood his ground, unwavering. Patty felt the grip around her hand slacken and the twisted shirt tails started to unfurl.

These soldiers were harder and more vicious than the marines she had known from the bases. There were no boundaries to limit or inhibit their reactions. With shaking hands, she unwound the shirt and smoothed it out. Soko left as quietly as he had arrived.

"Are you alright?" the captain asked, seeing the end of the confrontation. "What was that about?"

Patty choked up in the retelling and the captain drew her to him. "I'll talk to Henry. It won't happen again. But don't threaten them. They'll retaliate, and it won't matter that you're a woman."

"So, I'm supposed to let them maul me?"

"They were just blowing off steam." His dimples tweaked in a grin. "Can't blame the men because you're irresistible." His hand fondled her breast.

She hated that he assumed she was his property. His good looks or rank didn't give him the right to take what he wanted.

"You're hard to resist," he said and released her. "As much as I want to dip the wick, we don't have time."

Even though it was the '60s and free love was groovy, Patty had no intentions of letting him dip anything. But how could she stop him?

\*\*\*

They walked for hours through tall grass before coming upon the burned remains of a village. Patty tried to think of weapons that could cause this level of devastation. "What did that?" she asked.

The captain reached for the lighter in his pocket and ignited the flame. "It's a Zippo raid. Lots of crispy critters here." His silver lighter was smooth, with nothing engraved.

Critters! His words couldn't be erased from her mind. Women and children burned like weevils on cotton bolls. The captain stuffed his lighter back into his pocket as if this scene was of little consequence.

They continued walking through the blackened and ashen remains of people and reached the end of the scorched village. Patty wondered where the villagers who survived went. This was everything they had worked for all their lives.

Before the sun dropped its shadow over the earth, they ate by an imaginary fire. After the captain dug their foxhole, Patty laid out her poncho, snuggled into it, and tied up the grommets, encasing herself like a hotdog in a bun. He got in with his poncho and faced her. His hands undid her ties. Automatically, he reached for her breast. She tried to inch away when she felt his hand pushing between her legs and crawling up her inner thigh. She wasn't sure how to handle this. In another place and time, a slap across the face or kick to the groin got her point across. Here, she was afraid of these men and afraid to be on her own, but she wouldn't roll over for rape.

"This is the way it should be." His hot breath warmed her ear. "It was hard watching you with Soko last night. Why should I get the cold ground and him the prize?"

*Prize! Like I'm a thing to be used.* When Patty's hand massaged the muscle above his knee and moved to caress his thigh, she said, "My doctor told me that before I do it, I have to tell you I have gonorrhea."

His hand jerked from her inner thigh.

"It's not that bad. It's just that since this happened, I've been without my medication."

She could feel his body pull away from hers. She had got the idea from what that soldier said about a pecker checker. After watching army hygiene movies, Christopher and his buddies used to talk about gonorrhea. It was their big fear.

Relieved but not taking any chances, she continued. "This is the longest I've gone without my meds." She tried to sound apologetic and scratched her crotch to make the con more believable. "It's just that this time's the worst. They're working on a cure for it." The itch seemed unbearable.

"Get the fuck away from me and do those fucking grommets tight," he said, turning away.

Patty smiled thinking of the irony. She was a late bloomer. On the army base, her boyfriends had been too afraid of her father to go all the way. So, it was a year after she left home, that she had sex for the first time. The relationship lasted six months. And afterwards, she didn't have much time for dating between going to auditions, performing, working at the restaurant, and being an anti-war protestor. Most guys became frustrated with having to fit into her schedule and left. The odd one who hung around ended up becoming a lover. Sex hadn't been an issue then. And it looked like it still wouldn't be.

It wasn't long before Patty could hear the captain's slow deep breathing and knew he was asleep.

# Chapter 9

The captain poked her with the toe of his boot. "Get out of the fart sack."

Soaked in sweat, Patty kicked her leg trying to get the clinging rubber poncho off. Up in the trees, she spotted a bird with a green belly and a bright red streak on its head. Its constant call was unnerving. The urgency of its re-up, re-up, insistence was like a hysterical fast talker nagging her to hurry up.

The captain sent her off with his helmet and food packets to one of the fires. She made their breakfast and then dropped the wrappers into a foxhole beside the firepit. Pocketing the other treats and toilet paper from the accessory pack, she swished the helmet over the invisible flame.

After breakfast, Patty was cleaning out his helmet when the captain said, "Don't tell anyone you have gonorrhea." He sighed and shook his head. "Some prize."

*A prize you'll never get, moron.* She smiled, relieved that he wouldn't try anything again. Patty knocked the dirt off the rain ponchos, rolled them up, and put them in his rucksack. She was learning her duties.

"You're teamed with David, and you better hurry, because he's leaving without you," the captain said.

She rushed to catch up. It was about two hours before she felt brave enough to ask, "Where are we going?" When he didn't answer, she asked again. Stopping, he turned and scowled at her before continuing. His long deliberate strides forced her to jog. He never once looked back to see if she was still there. It was a struggle in the dense trees, but she kept on his heels, preferring to walk behind in case he triggered a booby trap. At least, that worry wasn't as bad now with his experienced pair of eyes watching out for them. It took the scaredness out of her step. She knew he was pushing her so he could complain that she couldn't keep up. But her legs were strong and used to five to eight hours a day of dancing. With men like him, one had to prove oneself.

After many hours, she had a spring in her step, whereas his pace had slowed from the weight of his pack. Glad not to be burdened by a heavy rucksack, she was often on his heels, pushing him harder. She spat out the gum and reached into her pocket for a cookie.

He turned around when she whispered his name. Wiping the crumbs from her face, she asked, "Can I have a drink?"

He leaned his six-foot-four-inch frame down to stare at her. She tried not to look at the blue thing that protruded from his eye. She didn't know if it was a vein or capillary that had bloated but it wasn't normal. She worried that the miniature blue balloon created a blind spot and then worried that he could miss seeing booby traps.

"Dagnabit—ears everywhere and you want to talk?"

She was surprised that he was winded.

After a slow deep breath, he exhaled. "I don't want to hear y'all breathe and if you so much as fart yur hist'ry."

He handed her his canteen and waited to get it back. Holding it to his lips, he took slow small sips, inhaling and exhaling with deep sighs. He tucked the canteen away and they continued in silence while life chirped and cawed around them. The mosquitoes didn't bother her as much since she had applied the bug juice. The forest was dense, and the trees were so tall, she felt dizzy trying to see their crowns. The blended squawking sounds were interjected by a loud shrill call—their signal. David spoke so low that Patty wondered if he only mouthed the word, "Skedaddle," when he pointed.

They jogged in the direction of the call and came upon the captain and his men standing around, while Soko sat on a rock strapping climbing spurs to his boots and lower legs. He secured a harness around his waist, then clamped a rope to it and walked around the tree roping himself around it. She watched as he lifted his foot, placed it onto the tree trunk, and did the same with his opposite foot. Leaning back, he flicked the rope up and used the harness and rope to leverage his weight as he walked up the tree.

"Why is he doing that?" Patty asked the captain.

The captain kept his eyes on Soko. "The trees are too tall for us to get our bearings, so he has to climb above them to pinpoint our location."

"You mean we're lost?"

The captain turned and looked at her. "No, he's doing it, so we don't get lost."

Patty couldn't believe how fast Soko was scaling the tree. "He makes it look easy."

The captain with his attention back on Soko said, "It is. The spurs do the work. Your body weight is more pressure than stomping your feet to drive them in."

Some men lay on the ground to look up. Soko rested for a short time at the top before he started his smooth and steady descent.

"The village is about one-and-a-half klicks to the north," Soko reported.

"Do we go around taking to the hills or through?" the captain asked.

"Through is faster."

"What do you know about these highland people, the Montagnards?"

Unclamping the rope and harness, Soko said, "They're our allies and most of them are Christian. We've recruited from a lot of the villages. There was a Montagnard massacre in Dak Son by the Viet Cong in '67."

The captain examined a stone on the ground, rolling it over with the toe of his boot.

"We don't know what we're up against in the hills, and time is tight. At least, we know the Viet Cong won't recruit from the village so snipers shouldn't be a problem. We go through." The captain had his orders relayed to the men.

The aquamarine sky and lush green landscape popped against the dull brown hues of the tilled soil, huts, and people covered in dirt and dust. Peasants stooping over their plot of land straightened up and tilted their wide-brimmed conical straw hats into the sun to look at the intruders.

Dirt had settled into the creases and onto their straight-legged cotton pants and plain long-sleeved shirts. A small-framed woman with a curved yoke around her neck teetered a bamboo pole and sloshed water from buckets at either end. Decrepit men walked out of bamboo-framed huts woven with tan and browned palm leaves. Children ran up with outstretched hands, begging.

"Okay, Salem." David reached into his pocket and threw Salem menthol cigarettes to them.

A girl about six ran in front of Shylock with her little palms out. He kicked her out of his way and sent her body sprawling onto the ground in a cloud of dust. Patty, the closest to him, threw her weight into Shylock's back. When he turned to confront her, she slapped him hard across the face and screamed, "Pig."

Shylock pulled his fist back. Henry intervened.

Shylock glared at him. "In my country, no woman would dare slap me. And the hand that struck me would be cut from her wrist so she could never disrespect me again."

Henry pushed his rifle hard into the man's chest. "Well, in case you haven't noticed, we're not in your country."

"You Americans are weak dogs. In my country, women know their place because men know enough to put them in it. No wonder you need my skills. You can't even control your women."

Overhearing Shylock, David nudged Soko, who was ahead of him in line, and relayed the situation. "He's mad as a mule chewing on a bumblebee."

Soko fell back, took Patty by the arm, and wedged her between himself and David.

The captain moved down the line of men. "No one fires unless fired upon."

Henry was the last person she had expected to help her. Maybe it wasn't helping her so much as putting Shylock in his place. No one seemed to like him.

"Watch them." David yelled as he pivoted his rifle in a semicircle. His tongue mimed the same action wetting the black bristles around his mouth.

A woman rushed to the girl, cradling her in her arms, rocking her as any mother would. Patty went to them, pulled out two tootsie rolls from her pocket, and gave them to the girl. The mother touched Patty's hand and nodded her head. The woman's dark eyes showed fear as she gathered the girl to her chest.

They walked away from the village without incident.

David leaned passed Patty to talk to Soko. "Dadgum, Shylock can speak English after all. And him ignorin' us all this time. Actin' like he couldn't understand when we was askin' him a question."

Soko looked back at Shylock who was walking by himself at the end of their line. "I don't trust him."

They continued walking for another four hours. At this time of year, the sunset was around 6:30 p.m. Patty checked her watch, 4:43 p.m. A short time later, the captain had the men make camp. Soko motioned for the captain to shadow him. They went farther into the bush.

\*\*\*

Patty kicked sticks and stones out of the way before she flicked the poncho into the air and watched as it covered the toe of David's black boot. Nervous and anticipating trouble, she looked for the captain, but he was nowhere in sight. Her unease grew as David watched her. She turned away and took a few steps then turned again.

"Y'all got a bee up your ass?" David's black brush cut and tanned skin were marked by gashes and scars.

"What?" Patty asked.

"Y'all got a problem?"

"What do you want?" Her voice trembled.

"Just obeyin orders."

Patty said, "The captain isn't here."

"I know." His tongue circled his lips. He stared up and down her length stopping at her breasts.

She folded her arms across her chest and turned to walk away. His calloused hand slapped down on her shoulder. "Yur not goin nowhere."

"Get lost." Patty pulled away. In doing so, her breast inadvertently touched his hand.

"Keep your redneck hands to yourself."

"Redneck?"

He looked angry.

"Them's fightin words."

He seized her arm and spun her back around. "I've met lots of highfalutin women like you. Thinkin yur too good for the likes of me. Thinkin I've got no sense on account of the way I talk."

Patty felt her cheeks flush when he let go of her arm.

"From a young'un, I was raised right. My daddy would have taken a switch to me if'n I treated a woman bad. But if y'all want a redneck, I'll get 'er done."

His grin looked cocky, and his posture changed. His shoulders thrust back, hands on hips. His accent became more pronounced. "I'd risk a switch to squeeze those melons of yurs, though. Out here, the only thin' a woman's good for is a nice piece of ass. And yur choice meat."

Patty noticed the other men laughing and watching as if they expected something to happen. Pressure built at her temples and worked across her forehead.

His tongue flicked into his beard. "I ain't about to do nothin. Don't get me wrong, it ain't like I don't want to ram it to you. There's just no sense me gettin my balls shot off, 'cause Soko's just mean enough to do it."

"What does he have to do with me?"

"He's why I'm here. Protectin the goods," he looked her up and down, "y'all might say. These gooks ain't too bright but leastways they know a woman's place is under a man's legs."

The other men laughed harder. Patty kept her eyes on the ground, afraid to look at him.

"That's the way it should be." He snorted and horked up.

Since she couldn't get away from him, she went back to the poncho and sat down. David followed and plunked his body next to hers. His smile showed crooked yellow teeth. Reaching for the captain's rucksack, she was quick to place it between them.

"Women nowadays got their nose in everythin and are too busy to satisfy a man right. And what with those women libbers, a home ain't a man's castle no more."

\*\*\*

When Soko was out of earshot from the camp, he continued. "I'm not sure what's changed between you and Patty. You don't seem to be bothering with her anymore. It's like you don't even want her walking beside you. The men will start thinking you don't care what happens to her."

"And they'd be right. Why should I care?"

"I know something has changed and I don't like where it's going."

"You don't like. Always trying to run the show, aren't you?"

"You've seen it the same as I have. After the killings, some men rape any woman close to them. It's like they get pumped up and have to release it."

"Yeah," the captain spat. "We got lots of them, double veterans."

"It could easily happen to her, especially if they think you don't care."

The captain smirked. "It burns your ass that I've got her, and you don't. You can't stand losing to me again." He chuckled. "You'd better get used to it."

Soko clasped his hands behind his back to stop himself from hitting him. "This isn't about you and me."

"Sure, it is. You're jealous. You can't stand that I got what you want. Just like with our careers. You were pissed off when they chose me over you. You can't stand taking orders from me."

"I don't care that you have her. I want you to show the men she's yours, so they keep their hands off."

"You don't get it, do you? I call the shots."

Soko made a long-exasperated sigh. "I know, you won. You beat me fair and square."

"Damn right." The captain leaned in closer to him.

"If you hear me out, I'll never question your orders again. Hell, I won't even compete against you for promotions."

"I like this side of you, Soko. Go on."

"If the men think you don't want her, they'll think she's up for grabs. They'll either fight over her or there'll be a gang bang. Either way, it could get ugly."

"What's the matter Soko, can't stand the competition or is it the sloppy seconds?"

"This doesn't have to happen. Her life depends on you."

"That's right, her life does depend on me. Because it's like this: the men in Washington can't afford any bad publicity about us fighting grunts. It's our job to make sure their asses are covered and to make them look good. So, if she's raped, she won't be going home to tell anyone."

"But you can stop it before it happens."

"We only need one compass here, so throw away your moral one. This is why they chose me. They know I'll cover their asses. I'm not going to let some cunt ruin my career. She'll just be another casualty of war, and what the men in Washington don't know won't hurt them."

"Then why bring her?"

The captain's stubby beard wasn't enough to hide the dimples that winked when he smiled.

"Because it pisses you off. She's my reminder to you that I'm in charge."

"Are you going to risk the mission on this shit?"

"The mission will go off without a hitch because it's my balls on the line. I'll do whatever it takes."

"Yeah, I know. You get rid of a problem instead of preventing it or fixing it."

The captain smiled. "And that's why the men in Washington love me. They can't trust you to do that."

"If they were in the trenches with you, they'd know what a fuck-up you are. Maybe the problem is there are too many guys in Washington like you."

"You're right. Maybe I do belong in Washington. By the way, we didn't have this conversation."

"Of course not. Why should we ever take responsibility for our actions? The end always justifies the means."

"A lesson you should start learning," the captain said and walked away.

***

Patty watched Soko stride into camp and forced herself to wait until he came closer. David got up and headed toward his poncho. She had hated walking in silence with David today, but now detested it even more when he spoke. She didn't understand why the men seemed to respect Soko and listen to him. When Soko saw her get up and come toward him, he turned around and walked away.

Patty chased him down and tugged his arm so he would face her. "Don't bother doing me any favors. The captain said I had nothing to worry about. I don't need your interference, so call off your redneck guard dog."

Soko laughed. "You didn't call him that, did you?"

"That's what he is. If you had the least bit of intelligence, you'd know the guy you picked to protect me is the one most likely to rape me."

"You don't have to be afraid of him."

His smile infuriated her.

"If he can't have you, he's going to make sure no one else does. It's always good to have him on your side."

"The man is despicable. He shouldn't be around normal people."

Soko laughed. "I've heard that said about him."

"The only one I need protection from is him. I don't know what you're setting me up for, but I don't like it or trust you. People want what they can't have. So, call off your guard dog. I've been around soldiers all my life."

"Not like these, you haven't. If you give them a nod, they'll take what they want."

"And what makes you so different?"

"Didn't say I was."

A strange, heady, dizziness engulfed her, causing her stomach to sink with the sheer disappointment of his words.

"This isn't Kansas, Dorothy, so wake up and smell the corpses. It's survival here."

Soko moved on to join Henry when he saw the captain coming.

*Isn't that just like a coward? As soon as he sees the captain, he turns tail and runs. He can't face a real man with power but likes to order others around.*

"Did you know that Soko had David guard me while you were gone?"

"No." The captain looked over at Soko.

"Am I in danger from your men?"

"You answered your question. They're my men. They do what I tell them."

"Well, someone should tell Soko that." They walked back to their ponchos.

Soko asked Henry what happened while he was gone. Henry laughed. "She shouldn't have called him a redneck. You know how he gets."

"Yeah, he's proud of his hillbilly heritage. Did he go on about not having much but it was enough, and about never accepting charity?"

"Nope."

"How about being God-fearing, and all about family, neighbors, and his dogs?"

"None of that. Didn't tell her he was from the Ozarks either. Went right into his redneck routine. You know him, 'if you want a redneck, I'll show you one.' Only, he really exaggerated it this time."

Soko laughed. "No wonder she was mad. Don't know why he thinks it's an insult to be called a redneck."

"It was prime stuff." Henry laughed again.

The captain made a fire and Patty cooked the pre-packaged meals one at a time. She fed him first. It wasn't done in a subservient way, although that was the way she thought he saw and liked it. She gave him the first serving, so his food would mop up the oil and dirt from his hair and the helmet would be clean to cook her meal. She knew now why the men referred to their helmets as pots. Pot head. The word came to mind and took on a different meaning that made her smile.

When she got up to get a large leaf to clean the helmet, she spotted Shylock staring at her.

Before darkness fell, everyone dug in for the night, including Patty. She needed to send a message to the men, so she dug her own foxhole—big enough for one small body. Her face and clothes were covered in the same dust that coated the others.

They settled in for the night. Two listening posts were set up with a man each, about a klick outside the camp's perimeter.

# Chapter 10

A boot rocked Patty's shoulder. She rolled on her back. "Move your ass." The captain dropped foil packets of food on her stomach.

The sun was starting to rise above the hills. Her long, slender fingers untangled knots and dusted off oily strands of hair. Listening to the captain instructing the men, she cooked breakfast. It would take her longer to fill in the foxhole than it would the men, so she had to eat quickly.

No time to exercise, she shook stiff muscles before heading out. Patty was walking with the captain. She was glad he hadn't paired her with David again. Closing in the perimeter, the captain kept the men within shouting distance. Patty perceived the approaching danger with each mile. The captain appeared tense. His strides were deliberate, his movements pronounced. Whatever these men were involved in, she was a part of it now. She tried to think of something else to take her mind off where she was. She liked to pretend that she was walking in the woods back home. It was easier now since the trees were shorter than the ones from yesterday.

When the captain stopped and inhaled deeply, Patty was curious and did the same. She couldn't smell anything. His face was scrunched up as if he was disgusted by something. He looked around. A few steps away, his gaze stopped on a boulder with a large fallen tree trunk beside it. He steered her in that direction. When they reached the spot, he pushed her to the ground, making the recognizable bird call. He elbowed her out of the way and rested his M60 machine gun on the boulder.

His chest was a veritable munitions dump of two hundred and fifty-round disintegrating, metallic split-link belts. Hand grenades and claymore mines were strung throughout his web-like vest. He unlinked the rounds of ammo that crisscrossed his shoulders and cocked the M60.

Crouching close to the rock, Patty's hands covered her head, body trembling. The first burst of gunfire surrounded them. Bullets ripped through the earth inches away. The captain unpinned a grenade and threw it. She heard the spray of dirt and debris after the explosion. He kicked Patty in the leg and shouted, "Hold the belt, feed the bullets."

She'd helped her father often with this. He'd taught her how the M60 worked and had fired it many times for her, never allowing her to do so. She was always his assistant feeding the cartridge belt into the gun.

Hefting the drooping belt, she held it level with the gun and fed it through. The rat-a-tat-dance of the weapon firing five hundred and fifty rounds per minute sent Patty's muscles into uncontrollable jerks and twitches. Its report sounded like grunts from a barnyard hog. Spent shells rained down around her. Gagging at the taste of sulfur, she coughed repeatedly. The earth rumbled from the undercurrent that vibrated with explosions.

To prevent the enemy from sneaking through the grass, the captain fired low. Not knowing how many enemy soldiers they were up against he didn't let up. She heard the kettledrum sound of a fifty-caliber machine gun behind them. A barrage of gunfire covering their backs gave her reassurance that help was here. Deafening explosions erupted. A spray of bullets whizzed overhead, and the captain's gun went silent.

Heat waves from the firing distorted her view. Gunsmoke billowed in thick clouds, reducing visibility. She was afraid to look sideways, afraid of what she would see. She turned her head, looked down, and saw his boot dig in like he was bracing himself. The captain reloaded.

Volley after volley, tit for tat, the captain gave as good as he got. Occasionally, his body jerked from the recoil. Gunpowder coated Patty's teeth, and the heat was suffocating.

His rapid-fire severed limbs from trees sending them crashing to the ground. Bullets ricochet off rocks and splintered shards of stone spiraled in every direction.

A sharp pain pierced Patty's side. She slumped and the belt of bullets dangled as a spot of warm blood soaked through her shirt.

"Put some pressure on it," the captain said.

Pushing a hand into her side, blood oozed between her fingers, dripping. She thought of Peter. The shock on his face. The holes blown through him. And the screams that she felt then, but couldn't release, came out now in long continuous wails. She drowned out the dwindling crack of gunfire until there was no other sound except her screaming.

"Let me see," the captain said, brushing away her hand. With a practiced touch, he swabbed away the blood.

She stopped crying. "How bad is it?"

"This isn't from a bullet. It looks like a rock fragment grazed your side. It's clean, nothing embedded. You've probably had worse skinned knees when you were a kid."

"Let me see," Patty said sitting up. Concern and worry were still etched on her face. "I'll need a bandage," she said.

"You can wait till we know if anyone has been hurt."

Guilt and shame made her snap back, "I didn't mean this minute."

***

When she watched Soko race toward them, she felt sheepish. After her gut-wrenching shrieks, he would have expected the worst and braced for the horror. The captain's body was in front of her blocking his view. When the captain asked if there were any casualties, he said, "I don't know. I came here first."

"Go check on the others," the captain ordered.

"She alright?" Soko stood his ground.

"I'm fine," Patty said, peeking around the captain's chest.

Soko left and returned shortly. "One wasted and one left arm T and T."

Patty didn't have to ask what wasted meant. "What's T and T?"

"Bullet entered and exited," Soko said. "It was nice and clean, through meat only, no bone."

When Soko came back to tend to Patty's wound, he brought a pair of North Vietnamese army boots and dry socks. He was surprised to see the size of the bloodstain on her shirt when he got out the medical supplies. "Lift your shirt and brace yourself. This is going to sting."

He seized both hands and pinned her with his elbow, then swabbed a burning trail of raw flesh. When he set her free, she punched him hard. His fingers stopped tearing at the packaging of field dressing, and he stared at her. The strong antiseptic smell misted her eyes, and her stomach tensed from the searing pain. Pulling the white gauze from the package, he applied it to her wound.

"Is it bad?"

"I wouldn't rush out to buy a casket. You've got plenty of time to shop around," he grinned. "The gashes you made from the leeches were more serious than this. Try these on." He handed her the socks and boots.

She knew he had taken them from a corpse, but she didn't care. She was glad to get them. Her running shoes had not come off since leaving Ca Lu, in case she had to run during the night. Water squished from the soggy runners and kept her socks damp. Her laces had been wet and dried so many times that the bow was stiff and hard to untie. It was a treat to take the stinking socks off.

Soko knelt beside her and lifted each foot to dry it on his shirt. He even dried between each toe.

It was too much of a coincidence that Soko had the same obsession as Peter, so she had to ask. "Why are you doing that?"

"If your feet are soggy for too long, you get immersion foot."

"What's that?"

"Your foot can absorb the sock. It's painful to cut the sock out of the skin. You're fortunate. There's no sign of it, yet."

She was putting on the boots when he said, "Tie your wet socks to the loops on your shorts."

When the captain gave the order to saddle up, Patty fell in line beside him.

"How did you know the enemy was there?" she asked.

"We can smell them."

She rolled her eyes.

"I really can smell the bastards. They use this shit called Nuoc-Mam on most of their food. It's an oily fish sauce that smells worse than garlic on a WOP."

Patty hated that derogatory name. She kept her eyes on the horizon to avoid seeing the corpses. Wriggling her toes into the dry, cozy comfort of her boots, she felt bad about punching Soko. Maybe he wasn't such a bad guy after all.

They jogged for an hour before slowing their pace to a brisk march for the next three hours. Patty was relieved to have the boots, especially when insects swarmed out of the marshy ground trying to bite her ankles in retaliation for disturbing their habitat. The deeper sections of the marsh, which the group avoided, sprouted the tops of partially submerged trees.

Heat came in rippling waves, making it difficult to breathe. They traveled in a straight line. The only noise came from the sucking mud as it oozed out from under their boots. After an hour, they trudged out of the marsh and were back on firm ground. Tall brush dotted the area, and men disappeared then reappeared at different intervals. They were coming upon a large section of elephant grass.

Patty's stomach grumbled and her legs were tired. The captain checked his watch. Happy to see his circular hand motion pointing a finger at the elephant grass, she knew they were stopping to eat. She stayed a few steps behind letting him blaze a trail through the tall grass until he stopped. The rest of the men kept in single file behind her.

The captain gave the order, "Nut to butt."

A tight circle forms through the thready grass. Bodies and faces emerged when rucksacks dropped, flattening out the grass.

Soko threw his poncho to Patty. "To protect your bare legs."

Sitting on those serrated edges of the elephant grass was painful. The grass acted like a wall around them. Everyone was busy rummaging through their packs for food.

The captain handed Patty a cloth-covered rice ball. He must have taken it off a Vietnamese corpse. She hadn't noticed him doing that. It must have been when Soko was dressing her wound. Her fingers rubbed the area. It wasn't hurting as much now. She watched the captain unwrap the rice ball and bite into it. She did the same. It was a treat to have fresh food.

They heard the engines first. Six planes flying in a single formation.

"Are they ours?"

"Does a bear shit in the woods?" David said.

"Those are B-52s," the captain said, checking his watch. "See the fighter coming up on the left? That's ours too. It's an F 105-D Thunderchief. They can—" All eyes watched as two planes exploded in a brilliant burst of white flames.

"Those whore'n Sams. Goddamn sons of bitches," Henry said.

"SAM, as in surface to air missiles?"

"Yeah," Soko supplied.

Black smoke tinted the blue sky.

"Saddle up," the captain ordered.

"Stay in line," the body behind her reminded. "Single file."

Walking out of the elephant grass, she saw the brush ahead and a forest beyond that. Brightly colored flowers looked like bouquets plopped between the greenery. Mushroom fungus nestled inside cracks on some trees while the bark of others was smooth. The rustle of leaves was constant, from monkeys swinging between branches. Their antics took her mind off her worries and let her enjoy the entertainment.

In the last three hours, the captain had checked his watch at least five times. This action reminded her of when he sniffed the air before the attack. He was anticipating something. It made her anxious. Each time he did that, she looked around ready to bolt behind a tree, and was relieved when it wasn't warranted. In the distance, a large expanse of burnt open ground with lots of craters appeared. They walked next to a hole that was big enough to conceal a jeep.

A ray of light glinted like sunlight reflecting off a mirror. The closer they got, the flashes became bigger and brighter. The jagged light splintering against blue sky reminded her of lightning before torrential rain on a humid summer's day. She knew the noise wasn't thunder. They were the same blasts from when she hid behind the waterfall.

They were headed toward the largest fireworks display she had ever seen. Mesmerized by shades and bursts of light through smoke, hours disappeared as they marched toward it. Again, the captain checked his watch. Patty wasn't sure if her body shook from blasts or fear. The men's movements looked disjointed between the brilliant bursts of light. She didn't understand why they were walking toward it.

The barren expanse of land in front of them had remnants of a leftover village. The captain pointed out large craters.

"They're made by thousand-pound bombs dropped by B-52s."

Even though there was no cover, the captain did that circular motion and stopped to give them time to rest.

"Where are we?" Patty asked.

The captain looked at his watch again. "The DMZ," he shouted into her ear.

"De-Militarized Zone! What are we doing here?"

"Crossing," he hollered back.

Patty waited for a lull between bombings. "You mean the border? Are you crazy? Why would we do that? We can't invade the north."

"We're not an army. Crossing the border doesn't mean invading them."

"Oh, excuse me, are we just going across to do a little shopping? Just because we're not wearing the uniform doesn't mean we're not American. As soon as they see us, they're going to know. Are you, spies?"

"No." The captain scowled.

"Why would we walk into this?"

He looked at his watch and then up at the bombers. "In exactly two hours and twenty-six minutes, the bombing will stop to give us enough time to cross."

She knew now, they weren't regular army and had to be some elite military group.

The captain checked his watch and shouted to the men, "Saddle up."

"No. I can't go."

"Not a problem," the captain answered. "If the bombs don't get you, the Viet Cong will."

"Where's the nearest base from here?"

"The enemy is nearest." The captain walked away.

She looked over from where they had come, then back and forth from there to the men who were heading out. She didn't want to run after them. But if she didn't go now, she'd lose them. With no map or supplies, she couldn't be on her own. She ran after them.

They walked for another hour and a half before the captain stopped to give them a ringside seat. The ground rumbled with vibrations that rippled her chapped, wrinkled skin.

Covering her hands over her ears, she looked around. The land didn't have the same dead quality that other lands had due to less devastation. It didn't seem right. Something was odd in how bolstered up it looked. Small patches of greenery sprouted. A simple country bridge over a river looked new and well-worn. There was a rice paddy but no huts or people.

Soko sat beside her and pointed to the ground. "We could be sitting on a village of a thousand people. Most underground villages have schools, clinics, a nursery, and recreational space."

He waited for quiet between blasts before speaking. "Tunnels connect the village to other villages." He looked up. "They sent Big Belly this time." Shielding her eyes, Patty gazed upward. The plane looked like a bigger version of a B-52.

Soko handed her a cloth to wipe the blood dripping from her nose and ears. "A hundred and eight bombs. That'll keep them underground. Even when the bombing stops, they'll know enough to stay put."

Patty looked up at the sooty sky.

To get her attention, Soko tapped her knee. "The Viet Cong come out at night to tend the crops and repair damage. We have to be gone and out of sight before nightfall. Can you hear me?"

Patty continued to stare at him. Her thoughts twirled in a vortex that matched the wild flashing bursts of light. When she wasn't rubbing her hands, she was biting her lower lip, chewing on it. *What was this mission? How could the government approve this? What if they were captured by the North Vietnamese?* She bit her fingernails. *Would they be tortured? Go to prison? How would they get out?* She rocked back and forth. *Would they be considered deserters or spies?*

# Chapter 11

The bombing stopped. The abrupt silence was startling.
"Saddle up," the captain ordered.

Patty stood up and trailed the men. She stopped when she saw the plane overhead, ready to run until the others waved at it.

"So far we're on target and intelligence was right." The captain faced the men. "Washington told us to expect little resistance. One skirmish, not bad. With forty-thousand North Vietnamese surrounding Khe Sanh, the border is vulnerable, giving us our window of opportunity."

Patty looked at Soko. "Forty thousand troops at Khe Sanh? I was trying to get there."

"Good thing you didn't."

"Let's go." The captain motioned with his arm. "We have to be gone before the North Vietnamese retreat and close that window."

It was a long and steady jog across the large expanse of destroyed land. There was a lot of time for Patty to question her choices. Obviously, going to Khe Sanh was not a good one. Maybe she should have left them the first day after meeting the group. The captain had given her a map and supplies. But what if she had gotten lost and ended up at Khe Sanh?

She worried about Christopher and wondered if he was alright. Da Nang was a huge base. Maybe they wouldn't attack it. She had been so close to where he was stationed and had hoped to see him soon. Now her chance was gone. If she got out of this, there was no way she was going back to the USO.

She thought of what this was doing to her dad. The things she should have told him. The fights they had when she was a teenager, bitter ones over Christopher going to war, and the last big fight about her joining the USO. The way she'd snubbed him. Making excuses to be away on special days. She knew he loved her. And she remembered all the good times with him. The things he taught her. Him, holding the back of her seat on the two-wheeler, running behind her while she grappled to stay balanced. Driving a jeep, the lessons with all the weapons and artillery. Hiking, camping, survival techniques, all the things she loved. Never one for parties, he preferred the outdoor life with his family. But the firing range was always their special time together.

Hours later, and clear of the DMZ, Patty was glad she didn't have a heavy pack strapped to her back. Sweat dripped from the men's foreheads. Their shirts were drenched and stuck to their chests. As afraid as she was of what these men would be doing, she was more afraid of being on her own. All she knew was that they expected to be rescued at some point and taken home. She presumed they were good at whatever it is they did.

They marched on, reaching a much higher elevation. Mountain range peaks came into view. The closer they got to the rock face, the thicker the brush became until they were encased in it. To help camouflage their point of entry into the thicket, and their subsequent trail, the men in the lead cut through the brush with their bodies instead of using machetes.

Patty held her arms up in front of her face ready to block any branches that sprang back at her. She squinted to protect her eyes from twigs that flicked off the branches like shards of splintered glass. One by one, the group came out of the thicket. They made their way through a small forest into the openness at the base of the mountain range. A rainbow overhead connected two peaks like a bridge to staggering layers of lush green. There was something about seeing those layered tones that filled Patty with hope. The view was vibrant and alive.

Trees rimmed cliffs that were cut from the sides of mountains. Two twelve-foot boulders had toppled to the base in some forgotten landslide. At the bottom, where the two rounded edges met the flat ground, was a perfect hiding place.

The men stood there a while, looking at the mountain before the captain had them turn back toward the forest and make camp. There was a quiet intensity in their mood. After dinner, the men gathered in a circle in a cleared-off area. Patty couldn't hear the words, but her dread intensified—instructions were being given. The men took things from their packs, obeying the captain's commands.

After a short time, the meeting concluded, and the men sat alone cleaning their weapons or re-arranging their rucksacks. They got rid of anything heavy, like extra water bottles or shovels. Because the ground was too hard nothing could be buried. They found hiding places in the bushes. No one spoke and the silence was eerie.

The evening turned to twilight and the setting sun went from a brilliant ball of orange to fuchsia, then to shades of apricot and lavender, and finally, it morphed into a deep purple.

Patty checked the illuminated hands on her wristwatch—7:18 p.m. Exhaustion soon knocked her out. Soko took the first watch. It was early into the night when he whistled their signal and slunk back into camp. Woken from a deep sleep, Patty wondered if she had dreamt of the sound. In the blackness, she thought she saw movement but wasn't certain. Blinking to bring clarity, she watched black forms slither behind bushes, logs, or large boulders. Then stillness. Soko's whispered signal caught her attention. Crawling over to her, he put his hand over her mouth. He undid the poncho's grommets and slid under the liner with her covering their bodies as a single light flashed.

Minutes went by before they heard the truck in the distance. A single beam from a light underneath the truck lit up the darkness ahead. The beam broken by trees flashed in long and short bursts, giving an illusion that Morse code was being signaled.

The sweaty poncho stuck to Patty. Soko's heaving breath cooled a spot on her neck. His steady puff of air contrasted with her irregular, ragged breaths. Soko removed his hand from her mouth.

Animals, startled by the noise of the truck, scurried into their hiding places. Patty lay as still as possible, but was annoyed when her body twitched. The sound of the truck diminished and darkness returned to the camp.

Patty whispered, "What's going on?"

"Transporting POWs probably."

"Where are they taking them?"

"Heartbreak Hotel or maybe The Hanoi Hilton."

"Prisons?"

"Hell holes. There could be more." They didn't move.

"Don't these people ever sleep?"

"Night's their best time. They torture prisoners for hours without getting interrupted. They bet on how much the guy can take and how long he'll last. It's easier to break a man in the dark. He can't see it coming—can't brace for the pain."

Patty was frozen by his words. His voice sounded haunted.

"Metal clicking—a knife sharpened—then a second of silence—when it's flipped over to do the other side." Under the liner, smothered by the heat, his voice trailed off. "You never know when or where," Barely audible his words seeped into the darkness. "Searing hot on bare skin," he breathed.

"We shouldn't have brought you." His words were only a breath. "Sorry, I didn't mean to scare you. There are a lot of guys looking out for you. You'll be fine. I have to get back to my post."

Patty didn't know how long she'd slept. Usually, she was a heavy sleeper. But something woke her. She had to pee. She tiptoed around the bodies. David's voice startled her.

"If yur takin a leak, go up yonder to the right."

She walked far enough away from his prying eyes and straining ears, unzipped, and squatted. Zipping her shorts up, she headed back to camp. She hated hearing the snap of twigs and imagined an animal crawling around her. The noise was minimal.

The force of an open hand slapped across her mouth and nose. The back of Patty's head slammed against a hard-muscled chest. No matter how hard she tried to breathe, only a trickle of air reached her lungs. Her ears were plugged. Everything felt compressed when she tried to swallow. Fingers dug into her cheek. Her hands clawed at the smothering hand. She felt his skin under her fingernails and a trickle of blood running down her arm.

Pinching her nose, he held tight on her mouth. Her arms fell by their sides, limp, and legs buckled. When he removed his hand, she dropped to the ground and breathed in hard as if drowning and had just broken the water's surface.

A cloth was stuffed into her mouth. It was warm with his sweat and tasted like Vaseline. Kneeing her in the back, he pushed her face into the dirt. He seized both her hands in his one fist. She felt wide tape being wrapped around her wrists and the jerk when he ripped the tape from the roll. Flipping her over, she saw the glint of silver duct tape in his pocket and recognized her assailant. Shaking her head back and forth, the tape stuck in her hair as he pulled a clump across her mouth and pasted it to her cheek.

Picking her up, Shylock threw her over his shoulder and carried her farther away. When he set her down, Patty tried to run but his large boot kicked her legs out from underneath. Her stomach muscles contracted from the air that was trapped behind the gag when she belly-flopped onto the ground. He rolled her over. With hands bound behind her back, she thought her arms would pop out of their sockets from the weight of his body on top of hers.

The burning in her shoulders shot across her back and down her arms. Struggling, heaving her body from side to side, she fought against him. In the dark, she couldn't see it coming, but the punch split her lip. Buttons popped from her shirt when he tore it off. Sitting on top of her, he sniggered as she kneed him repeatedly in the back. She felt him grab his crotch massaging it, moaning. He was getting a thrill from her fighting back. So, Patty lay still. His knuckles connected with her cheek sending a searing pain to her eye.

Shylock's lips touched her ear. "You American women are pigs. You won't fight to protect your honor."

In some sadistic foreplay, he caressed his knife blade against the swollen cheek, down her neck, between her breasts, and then cut into the crisscross of the Wonderbra.

With the gag filling her mouth, snorting up his putrid body odor, Patty turned her head when his face almost touched hers. "American women need to be shown their place. No woman interferes with what I do. You are no better than my dog. You live if I decide it. I will teach you my country's law and soon your offending hand will be no more."

\*\*\*

David came to relieve Soko from sentry duty. "I don't know why one dadgum person has to make so much noise just takin a piss. A bear shittin in the woods is quieter."

"What are you talking about?"

"Patty. She went for a piss. But she's been gone long enough to drip dry."

"I'll check on her," Soko said.

"I told her to go right up yonder," he pointed.

\*\*\*

Shylock slid the knife down her ribs to her belly button. The knife jumped each time her stomach muscles flinched. His body shook with silent laughter. Patty closed her eyes and stiffened as she felt the cool blade slide up the leg of her shorts. It scratched her inner thigh. She was afraid to move—to fight back. She opened her eyes when the tip of the blade pricked the skin as he lifted the knife to cut the shorts.

Suddenly, Shylock's body sprawled sideways as a sledgehammer fist drove into the side of his head. Curled into a ball to hide her nakedness, Patty heard the grunts between punches. The scuffle of bodies and boots kicked up dirt and dust. Then one loud blow led to silence. A dark figure moved toward her, picking up the fallen knife enroute, standing overtop.

"It's me, Soko," he said kneeling, adjusting his night goggles that had gone askew in the fight. Taking off his shirt, Soko draped it over Patty's shoulders. He sat her up and used the knife to cut the duct tape from around her wrists.

"There's no easy way to take duct tape off. Normally, I rip it off quickly." He snapped his fingers in front of her eyes. "Hey, hey are you with me?"

He jiggled her shoulders. "Just shake your head. I need to know."
She shook her head, yes.

"Don't need hysterics, not now. Okay, I'm going to go slow and easy." He gently tugged on the tape holding the skin around it. She didn't flinch when he pulled strands of hair from her head. All she felt was numbness.

"Sorry," he said when he saw the clump of hair stuck to the sticky underside of the shiny silver tape.

Her chin rested on her chest.

"Stop feeling sorry for yourself. If you want to feel sorry for someone, think of the kids that go through this and are raped. There's no one to rescue them." He freed the tape from her cheek and hair.

Lifting her head, she glared at him, feeling her teeth grind between the balled material.

"Anger's good. I'm going to take this rag out of your mouth. But don't make a sound." Reaching into her mouth, he pulled out the wadded material. Tears streamed down her cheeks as her lips quivered holding back silent cries.

"This will never happen again. We're here to protect you."

The horror of it all was too much. Patty was afraid if she opened her mouth, she would let out terrifying screams. So, she stayed quiet. Afraid.

"Do up the shirt. I need to know you can function."

She understood what he was saying, but doing anything seemed overwhelming. She just sat there.

"Move, so I know you're with it. You have to get through this or you won't make it out with us."

Those words got her attention. With shaking hands and much difficulty, she slid into the shirt and did up the buttons.

Soko walked over to where Shylock lay moaning. He thumbed the safety off his pistol and kicked the soldier's leg. "Get up."

The silver glint from the duct tape hanging from Shylock's belt reflected in Soko's goggles. "Stand up, hands on your head." He shoved Shylock in front of him and they walked over to where Patty crouched.

"Get behind me," Soko ordered her, and the three walked back to camp.

The captain awoke, reaching for his gun, when they walked up to him. "Who the fuck is there?"

"It's Soko. I've got Shylock and Patty."

The captain sat up and put his starlight scope goggles on. Soko's gun was still on Shylock.

"What the fuck did you do to him?"

"Not enough."

"You know how important he is to this mission?"

"That's why he's still alive. I couldn't stand there and watch him rape her."

"You could have joined him for all I care. The fucking bitch has gonorrhea. She's a diseased whore."

The captain's words struck Patty like another blow and started another stream of silent tears.

"He'd better be able to climb tomorrow, or you can say goodbye to your career."

"I'd do it again if I had to."

"You can't leave things alone, can you?"

The men closest to them were awake and listening to the confrontation. No one spoke.

"This is fucking great," the captain complained. "Just the time we all need a good night's sleep, this fuckup happens. All of you, get some sleep." He rolled over and turned away from the group.

When Shylock walked away, Soko didn't stop him. He wrapped his arm around Patty's back. She made no noise, but from her shaking back and irregular breathing, he'd know she was crying. She tried to hide it. Show him she was tough. But her body gave her away. He walked her to where he had left his poncho, collected it, and walked to where she had bedded down. He spread out his poncho next to hers. He was close enough to whisper in her ear, but he didn't touch her.

"Take a deep breath," he instructed. "Now, let it out slowly. Another deep breath," he counted down the seconds before he said, "Exhale." He repeated inhale, the countdown, and then exhale, several times, until her breathing was rhythmic and the tremors that raked her body disappeared.

Exhaustion, and knowing she was safe for now, let Patty fall into a deep sleep. Sunlight inched its way into the black sky. The coolness in the damp ground started to warm from the intensity of the spreading rays. Patty was stiff and sore as she looked around at the men eating. She licked her swollen lip, and her tongue touched a rough scab that had formed over the split. Seeing Shylock, she was surprised that she wasn't afraid of him. She hated him so completely, it took away the fear.

Even though Shylock had checked his weapons and ammunition the previous night, he re-checked them again. It infuriated her that he was allowed to go about his business as if nothing happened. Patty hoped his head was throbbing. Soko was right. It could have been worse.

Soko walked over to her and handed her two foil pouches of cooked oatmeal and a canteen of water. "You're going to need it to keep up your energy."

She saw the worry on his face and in his eyes. "I'm alright, thanks to you."

"Let's see your hand."

Patty turned her palm up. He unwrapped the dressing. "That's healed nicely. The wound cream works wonders. How about the gash on your stomach?"

"It's good. Already has a scab. It doesn't hurt anymore."

"That's good 'cause it's going to be a hard day."

She felt the scab on her lip with her tongue and sucked on it.

"Don't worry, it feels worse than it looks. You're still pretty under the bruising and dirt." He left her to eat while he dealt with his rucksack. When Soko returned, Patty was rolling up her poncho.

"You won't need it."

"Why not?"

"Can't tell you."

"Are you leaving me behind? It wasn't my fault. It was Shylock's."

"We're not leaving you."

She pulled up her shirt collar, dried her unexpected tears, and covered her sob with a quick swipe of her hand.

Soko snapped a carabiner and lanyard onto her belt loop and attached a canteen.

"Saddle up," he said, before strapping on his rucksack.

It was surprising how quickly the landscape changed from jungles, swampy marshes, rugged terrain, forests, to mountains. Walking back to the mish-mash of high and low mountains, Patty faced their imposing lush green walls. It was hard to discern which stone was under this thick covering of greenery that clung, draped, sprouted, and embellished either limestone, sandstone, or granite.

Soko walked over to where David was sorting his gear. Patty had a suspicion they had arrived at their secret destination. Her stomach lurched. She couldn't face her fear of heights. She wouldn't be able to do this.

# Chapter 12

I hate that I can't cook my meals, clean my house, and even look after myself without a personal support worker. They give me showers, wash my hair, and do all the things I can't. Getting old is the shits, literally. But the good thing is, you can say what you want, living life without a filter. That's why I like the internet. I'm anonymous. People listen, and I can debate my points. I'm heard. My profile is a cat and my name, is Say Cheese.

When I get the last word, it could be my last word. Got to make it count. Problem is, no one cares what old people think—including our daughters. Can't let them rule my roost. This is one hen who knows how to keep foxes from invading my house. I'm not going without a fight.

I don't want to go into the home. "I'll lose who I am." These words give me that Deja Vu feeling. It was over fifty years ago when I first heard them. Soko said them and those same words were written in Christopher's letter. If I remember this, then I can't be losing it, can I? Now I know how they felt. I don't want to go to the home and lose who I am. Living by someone else's rules.

My children's questions are like an interrogation. They put me on the defensive. Am I eating right—they check the fridge. Have I been to the doctor lately? Is the house getting too much to look after? They check my kitchen cupboards for food and my bathroom for Depends and wonder if I'm losing it. They already took my car.

They must have read the latest magazine article on how to determine if your loved one is senile or developing Alzheimer's. A test to tell when it's time for the home. A score to determine my fate.

As they were growing up, how many times did I have to ask for something to be done, to hear, "Sorry Mom, I forgot." Now, God help me when I forget. It seems I'm not allowed. If I forget anything, they whisper, "She must be losing it." I don't want to be pushed out of my home. It's where I can still feel Soko's presence. I'm afraid to leave him. I don't want to be alone. I was never any good at facing my fears—not without Soko.

***

Patty faced the mountain. "I can't do that."

The captain shrugged. "Then there's nothing we can do for you. I guess this is where we part company."

Soko overheard their conversation and walked up to them, with David trailing.

"You knew it was going to come to this. Why bring me?" Patty said.

The captain put his hands on his hips. "You're the one deciding, not me."

"We'll take her with us," Soko said.

The captain dropped his rucksack. "It's too dangerous. I can't allow it."

"I can't do this," Patty said.

She was surprised David didn't protest, his look was dirty.

Soko clamped his hand on the captain's shoulder. "She stays with me."

The captain knocked his hand away. "It's your career and your funeral." He picked up his rucksack and left. David walked back to his gear.

"It's small." Soko shaded his eyes surveying the mountain. "A good one for beginners."

"Doesn't look small to me. How long will it take to climb?"

"Considering our heavy packs, probably about thirty minutes for each mile and sixty minutes for every two thousand feet of ascent, so about five hours. But with a beginner, your guess is as good as mine."

"I'm afraid of heights," she said.

He turned and faced her. His fingers bit into her shoulders. "You can do this. You have strong arms and legs and great balance."

"No, I can't," her voice trailed off into a whimper.

"You have no choice."

She knew he was right.

David was ready to go. With the safety on, he attached his M16 to his harness and walked to where they stood.

"Let's go," Soko said, prodding Patty up the mountain base with David on her heels.

She concentrated on the climb. The first part wasn't as bad as she'd imagined. She'd hiked up hills with her father often. But nothing near as high or as dense with foliage. She knew how scary it could get, the higher the climb. Soko was right. She shouldn't look up or down. It got her imagining the worse. For right now, this was good.

There were so many bushes, trees, and rocks, there was always something close by to hold onto when the going got steep. The ground was soft with chipped bark and spongy moss. Decades of fallen trees had splintered against the chiseled stone and littered the ground with kindling in various stages of decay.

Patty was careful to step on the stone, afraid that her foot would sink into the mulch and get wedged between hidden rocks. Some animals and plants were new to her. She almost slipped off a large moss-covered rock when an odd-looking rabbit hopped out from under an evergreen tree. The animal had tiger-like striped markings and a red rump. It was hard to concentrate on the climb with the distractions of animals, foliage, brilliantly tinctured orchids, and other flowers.

"Keep going," Soko prodded. "We're about a third of the way there."

She quickened her pace through the easier terrain to help make up for the time they would lose on the difficult parts. Her body craved this exertion and she was feeling pumped. That was why she loved sports dancing and hiking.

Walking in a deep ravine, Patty asked, "What kind of rock is that?"

"Limestone," Soko explained, wiping the sweat dripping off his nose. The heat caught between the craggy blue-grey stone was like a sauna. Seeing this beauty, she had forgotten they were in a battle zone until arriving upon a huge expanse of stoney barren land. Like a lumpy bald spot on a thick head of hair, it looked out of place.

"Bombs." Soko slapped a big flat limestone boulder. Their blasts had scarred the land. "We'll rest here."

Covered in thick flora, it offered a nice cushion. Vines hung from the sides touching the ground. There was enough room for all three of them.

"It's going to be more difficult from here," Soko said, handing Patty some beef jerky and a water canteen. The ground was stoney. "We'll be scrambling now."

She took small swallows to avoid hiccups and stomach cramps. When her jerky was done, she wiped her lips with the back of her hand, careful not to scrape the scab. She handed the canteen back.

He took a swig. "At least the weather is cooperating. It's clear, with little wind. Good thing it's the dry season."

She'd scrambled before with her dad on stone. But not for this distance. And it had been on shale that he called scree. *Strange name scree. Could never figure that one out. Probably a joke. 'Cause I did scream. The last letter falling off scream like a person off a mountain.*

Scrambling made sense. She'd put her hands down and steadied herself to move upward. Hunched over like a bear, she walked on all fours over rock, scrambling up steep terrain.

But it was the rock climbing that terrified her. She'd never done that before. Nothing straight up where she had to use her hands and pull herself up. And this mountain was much bigger than anything she'd scaled. *Too late to worry now. Worry. Odd what a word could trigger. Peter. Their hike. His words. The more you worry, the worse it gets.* She shook her head, as if by doing that, she could fling the thoughts out before remembering his death.

Soko stood up and tightened his rucksack. "Time to go."

She looked at David who was doing the same. If the pack wasn't secure, it could flop from side to side putting her balance off. That was the first thing her father did for her before scrambling. She didn't interrupt Soko when he went over the tips. She knew how to slant her foot for a firmer stance or to use the toe of her boot to push off, but it was good to get a reminder.

The climb was slower now and more grueling than she'd imagined. The sun's intensity made her think it was around noon. Sweat soaked her shirt. Patty held on and stopped to catch her breath, watching David hop up onto a large boulder. She would have to go around it when she got there. He prowled from rock to rock like a sure-footed animal with a gliding motion.

She felt clumsy. Taking her time deciding which rocks were more secure. Testing them first to make sure her foot wouldn't roll. It was a relief to know Soko was behind her in case she slipped. Her legs and arms ached. Just when she thought she couldn't go on, the landscape changed again and they could walk upright once more. It was a long trek. Her foot rolled on loose stone putting off her balance. But Soko was there to steady her. He dropped her hand. Pulling out his pistol, he attached a silencer. Patty followed his aim. A weird animal ran across the stones and stopped when it spotted them. It appeared to be a cross between a wolf and a fox. They all remained still until it sprinted off.

The farther they walked, the less stone covered the ground.

"Trees been clear cut," David said.

"Yeah. Probably an army operation," Soko explained to Patty. "We use them for fuel."

He turned again to David. "Or maybe for access to the north? Suspicious, that it's in the direction of the fortress. Must have been our guys."

The elevation was rapidly changing, with rises becoming steeper.

"We'll have to climb from here." Soko looked at David. "You take the lead, then I'll follow and Patty you'll be tied in at the end of the rope."

"Can't I go in the middle? I'd feel safer," Patty said.

"You weigh a lot less than David, so I have to belay him. David will be putting pitons into the rocks, and I'll be taking them out as we go, so we can reuse them. Being at the end, you don't have to worry about any of that."

"The pitons aren't meant to help you climb. It's protection in case of a fall. When David reaches the anchor at the top of the first pitch— a pitch is the length of the first section of the climb—he'll attach himself to the anchor and then become our belayer from above. I'll reach David at the first anchor and secure myself to it and David will continue belaying you so you can anchor in as well. Then the process repeats. We stay tied in and David leads again. You won't have to belay anyone. He does it from the top and I do it from the bottom."

Patty felt her stomach sink and tighten at the same time. Soko threaded the one hundred and ninety-seven feet of nylon rope through his hands.

"You take the sharp end," Soko said to David.

Her face must have given away her confusion.

"It means David is in the lead."

She watched David make loops and knots twirling rope and attaching it to metal rings that he clamped onto his harness. Soko turned her around and tied her hair into a ponytail with a piece of cord using a figure-eight knot. When he turned her back around, they looked at each other—a silent moment passed between them. Soko squeezed her hand.

"Since you're at the end, you won't have to belay. But watch me and see how it's done."

Sizing up that mountain brought back her fear of heights. "I can't. I can't," she cried.

He hung his head and closed his eyes as if in pain. Letting out a deep sigh before opening his eyes, he said, "The North Vietnamese offer a twenty-five-thousand-dollar reward for white women."

Patty's tears stopped when her mouth gaped wide. "Ten thousand." The words came out in a whisper. "That's what the army thinks I'm worth. That's the life insurance they gave me."

He took her hands and tugged her toward him. "You have no choice. If you stay, they'll find you. They'll think you have information and torture you."

Soko adjusted his gear. Weapons hung off anything that could be clipped to his rucksack, web gear, or harness with rope and carabiners. He took a couple of steps to where David was assessing the route.

David nodded, "I'm good." He started his ascent.

Tucking his shirt in, Soko said, "So I don't get rope burn."

Patty had watched the other teams starting their climbs. They were the only team left on this flatter ground. She felt bad. It was her fault. They'd been held up with all the instructions Soko had to give her.

Soko headed up. The rope near her feet lifted from the ground and trailed him in a straight line. She moved to see where he was putting his hand and footholds, and instantly regretted it. Dirt dusted her face from his shifting weight. This was why Soko had told her not to stand directly under him. She rubbed her eyes repeatedly trying to get the grit out. Tears puddled under her bottom eyelashes held there by her swollen cheek. She flushed her eyes with water and kept blinking. *Just great! Haven't even left the ground and I've already screwed up. What are the chances…Stop worrying.*

She tried not to rub her eyes and continued blinking. By the time she felt the tug on the rope, her eyes felt better and had stopped watering. Eaten away by nature, numerous, large, pieces of rock made for great hand and footholds. There were many wide ledges and deep cracks, always something within easy reach. Attached to the rope, she felt more secure. Maybe this wouldn't be as bad as she had imagined. Patty understood the danger. Rock climbing was life or death, and a beginner offset the odds.

She'd made it. At least to the first anchor. Soko transferred the pitons back to David's harness for him to then repeat the process. She had no idea how many more times this would happen until they got to the top.

Anchored in, she watched David and then Soko climb. She couldn't believe how fast and far Soko was already. This wasn't anything like scrambling. It felt good to be standing up straight and not hunched over. Remembering Soko's step-by-step instructions and his relaxed tone helped drown out hysterical thoughts as she climbed. Taking a breather, with both feet planted, took the pressure off her limbs before she continued.

At the next pitch, David hollered to her, "Piece a cake, right? This here's a righteous trainin ground. Ready?"

Patty glared at him and gritted her teeth. David didn't wait to hear her answer. On the move, his hands and feet easily found solid holds. Soko was next up and soon became a distant figure. Feeling a slight quick double tug, she knew it was her turn now.

Reaching up with her left hand to get a firm grip, she peeked down for a likely foothold. Spotting one, she lifted her right leg and scraped her knee against the rough rock. She placed her foot into a wide crack and tested it with her weight. The same process was repeated for her opposite hand and foot. She couldn't have imagined making this climb in her soggy running shoes. The boots gave her traction, and the deep treads were something to hold on to. Soko must have been thinking about the climb days ago when he got her the boots.

Inch by inch, she made her way upward, wiping the sweat from her forehead with her arm. She concentrated on what she was doing and didn't check out the impossible climb ahead or look down past a foothold. Glancing across, she watched as she passed one of the other climbing teams taking a rest on a wide ledge. She took a deep breath, aware that they must be watching her clumsy attempts, happy that she wasn't part of their team.

She was tired and wanted to stop but knew she shouldn't. Her hand reached up close to a ledge and she felt Soko's large hand wrap around her wrist in a firm grip. Climbing up one more foothold, she was able to boost her body onto the platform with his help. He didn't let go of her wrist until her feet were firmly planted on the large flat surface.

Patty didn't smile or scowl. Not even her eyes flickered an emotion. Her chest heaved in and out in time to her puffing cheeks.

"You did friggin' good," David said, as she rested, hands on knees, with head down. Sitting on the rock, she sat with back against a boulder.

"Didn't I tell y'all this was gonna be a breeze? We're makin good time. Better than I thought. That other team was eatin' our dust. I ain't never been last in anything. Seems like we're still not gonna be."

*Where was the crude obnoxious redneck I'd come to know and hate?* His enthusiasm was lost on her. There was enough space on the mantelshelf for Patty to lie down. Shielding her eyes from the sun's glare, she focused on the incline. She closed her eyes, listened to her breathing, and wondered how they could make it up from here.

"Don't fall asleep," Soko warned. "You'll feel better if you sit up and stretch your leg muscles. Put your legs straight out, point your feet down, then straight up."

Patty mimicked his commands.

"Keep repeating that and hopefully, your muscles won't cramp."

The occasional cold gust of wind was refreshing. She laid back on the stone, fed up with exercising. Not wanting to hear anything more about the climb, she closed her eyes. She knew she wouldn't fall asleep. The rock was too hard. She felt like she'd been still for too long. Her breathing was normal, but her body seemed to be in overdrive. Muscles tingled with a hyperactive response to the danger ahead. She opened her eyes and stared at the massive wall.

"It's steep, but it's not straight up. It's a small mountain. You'll be fine." Soko reassured her.

# Chapter 13

D avid started his ascent with Soko belaying him. Before beginning his climb, Soko gave her a stick of gum.

"Make sure you test each foothold and ledge before you put your full weight on it. Keep to the right of me and not directly underneath," Soko said.

"Yup. I learned that one already," Patty said.

Feeling the tug on the rope, she lifted her left hand, then right foot, right hand, and left foot. Grasping a jutting piece of rock above her head, she pulled herself up. Peering down, she ran her boot along the rock until she felt a foothold. She kept repeating the process until she was about half the distance from the rope. Footholds had turned to toeholds. Midway, when she lifted her left foot, the top of her boot scraped against a protruding ledge. She steadied herself and tried again. Putting her left foot on a shelf, she tested it. With the sound of crumbling stone, the mantel shifted, and she screamed, "look out," forgetting there was no one behind her. It sounded like gravel being poured. Her heavy breathing made her tongue feel thick. She was glad for the gum. Stiff and rigid from tension, fatigue set in. The tightness in her muscles brought on cramping in her secure foot. There was no place to rest. She had to keep moving.

Even though it was cool, her legs were itchy from sweat. She slid her foot to the side hoping to find the assurance of a safe foothold. There was nothing. Jabbing and poking at the rock, trying to regain a footing, her body teetered until she felt a wide ledge. She put her full weight on it. The ledge crumbled into nothingness. Pitched forward, the other foot was pulled from its secure hold. Both legs dangling, Patty's fingers held tight to the rocks above her head. Dry mountain air wheezed in and out of her lungs. Her arms ached. Patty's fingers peeled off the wall. She had no breath to scream. An echo from her forgotten past triggered a silent Geronimo—oooh. A word from childhood—reliving the fear.

\*\*\*

Eleven years old, she stood on the squat shed roof with her friends. She'd been up and down the roof more than ten times, jumping off and screaming "Geronimo." She'd done it hundreds of times before. She walked to the edge of the roof, ready to jump when her friend grabbed her arm, pretending to push her over the edge, then jerked her back. It created a fear that never existed before and it panicked her. All afternoon Patty watched her friends jump off the roof. She sat on the rough shingles while her friends came back up to do it again and again. When the streetlights came on, she had to get home for supper. She walked to the edge of the roof. She couldn't do it. None of her friends could coax her down.

A rescue plan was hatched. Tommy Forte got an orange skipping rope. He tied it around his waist. Since he was the biggest kid there, he became the anchor at the end. Tommy told Patty to lie face down. He threw her the yellow handle at the other end of the skipping rope. The other three friends hung onto the skipping rope to help Tommy hold her weight. Patty's knuckles bled from the rough shingles as they lowered her down.

\*\*\*

She fell straight down the mountain without struggling. The abrupt jerk from the rope squeezed around her waist pinching her skin. The gum flew from her mouth. Jolted by the sudden stop, her breath cut off. Her torso flopped over and her head went between her legs. She awoke still too stunned to know what was happening. Hearing her name called, she lifted her head as blurry shapes slowly became recognizable. Soko was above her, hanging from a piton anchored into the rock. He was swinging her rope. She must have fainted. Hefting her body upright, her mind focused on the reality of her plight.

"You have to help me," Soko said. "You have to swing yourself back to the wall."

His tone was calm and reassuring. "Come on, it's easier than you think. You probably did this as a kid jumping from a rope into the lake."

*Yeah, I did that all the time at the cottage.*

"I'm going to help you by pulling the rope. Push off with your feet and catch the wall on the next swing."

Concentrating on the wall, Patty decided on a point that offered the best opportunity from where she was. Spotting a protruding hunk of rock with enough room for footholds, she made that the target. Being focused on the target slowed her breathing and made her calm just like when she had pulled the trigger at the shooting range. Patty's body moved with the rhythm of the rope, gaining momentum, reaching both hands out, pushing harder, getting closer, her fingertips almost touching the stone. The next swing brought her in close enough to reach the wall. She pushed harder in sync with Soko's moves, her eyes never leaving the target, and grasped the rock pulling her body in close. Her feet were firmly planted without her knowing she had positioned them there.

"Stay calm. You're in a good spot. And I've secured you. Now's the time to rest. Deep breaths in and out," he said.

*I did it. Far out. Cool. Thought I was a goner.* Her fingers gripped tighter on the stone. *Figured I'd be a splat on the rock. It's doable. Just hang loose.*

"Now you know the worst that can happen. You're not going to plow into the ground if you slip free. If you struggled, you could have gotten tangled in the rope, flipped upside down and smashed against the rock."

He gave her time to recover. "Legs feel strong enough now?"

"Yeah. I'm good."

"Okay. Remember, always test the footholds."

He was once again climbing while she rested, waiting her turn. The tug on the rope was sooner than she had anticipated. She took her time and became more sure-footed. Having experienced the worst and survived, panic left her step. It took them two more hours before David reached the top of the mountain. When Patty was close to the top, Soko leaned over the edge, reached down with his hand, and helped her up. Standing on the flat ground beside her, the two men gave each other a smile and a nod. They were the last team up.

The mountain ended in a forested plateau. The other men were scattered about. Patty undid the swami belt and handed it to Soko. She needed to get away from the edge. Standing far enough away, she was surprised that panic hadn't consumed her when viewing the beautiful scenery below. But her legs still felt rubbery. As Soko ditched their climbing gear, Patty stomped away, bringing feeling back to her legs.

The men crouched low under the shade trees and re-organized their rucksacks. Patty took the canteen Soko offered her and found a shade tree to lie under. The leaves swayed with a gentle breeze, and, for the first time since the climb began, she could relax, and her breathing slowed to a normal pace.

"You nearly killed them," the captain said, squatting down beside her.

She kept her eyes upward. Just the sound of his voice irritated her. She wanted to hit him. Smash that pretty face so he appeared as ugly as he really was.

She regarded him and smiled. *When the time's right, you'll get yours.*

Patty remembered her father saying, "You could always tell a good officer by the mutual respect expressed between him and his men." The captain demanded respect but never gave it. He only gave orders. Maybe her father hadn't been the Hitler she'd accused him of being in her teenage years. After walking a mile in his shoes, she was beginning to understand him. Maybe their relationship had a chance. It took a war to break them up. It seemed appropriate that the same war should bring them together. Soko dropped his rucksack and sat down beside her. Foraging through it, he took out packets of dried fruit, nuts, and oatmeal chunks, handing them to her. When she reached for the packets, he examined her hands which were red from the climb. His hands were calloused. She imagined nothing affected them. And he had said, this was one of their easier climbs.

She leaned against the tree trunk and opened a wrapper. "So, what's the plan?"

Soko got out the wound cream. "You'll be up close and witnessing a battlefield."

Patty stopped chewing on the piece of dried fruit.

He stared at the red gummy fruit stuck to her teeth and she quickly closed her mouth.

"We'll keep you as far away as we can, but you'll still have to be close for a speedy getaway."

"So, climbing was the easy part?"

"Yeah."

"This is why you didn't want me to come? Why you were arguing with the captain?"

"Yeah. I don't know why he changed his mind. He made the right decision that first night."

"Maybe it was because I saved his life. The enemy I killed was going to kill him."

"Well, he didn't do you any favors."

Patty ate, feeling comfort from the food, and her stomach stopped grumbling.

Soko took both her hands and turned their palms up. "How are they?"

"Burning."

He applied cream and bandaged them. "It'll take a few hours, but the burning should go away. You need to get some sleep."

"Are you kidding me? After what you told me."

"It's going to be hours before we pull out."

"I'm sorry for giving you a hard time. I was mad at you for not letting me come."

"Yeah, I know." He cupped his hands around her face careful not to touch the bruise. "You need to rest."

He put his arm around her back and slid their bodies down along the grass until they were lying down. Patty turned her body toward him and laid her head on his chest. He massaged up and down her back. With her tense muscles relaxed, it felt like she was melting into him.

"You did good, conquering your fear like that. Never met anyone like you."

"You don't climb mountains with other women?"

"Most women I date are caught up in shopping and the nightclub scene. Neither interests me. It's frivolous compared to the military do-or-die lifestyle. Can't relate to them. Being home is going from one extreme to another."

Patty raised her head to observe him. "So, what's your type?"

"Someone with opinions, and global views, so we can discuss things; a person with scruples and convictions who will take a stance on issues. The women I've met are all fluff and no stuff."

Patty had never been able to sleep during the day. Not knowing what would happen, how she would react, or even if she could, kept her tossing from side to side. She tried not to disturb Soko who seemed to be sleeping. Her body tingled with pins and needles, making it impossible to rest. She must have slept at some point because when Soko nudged her, she woke with a snort. *How attractive.*

The sun had started its rapid descent. Nature's talented hand used the largest canvas possible to ridicule man's rule of pigment combinations and brushed bold strokes of pink and orange beside the red fireball. Trees had become black shadows that made small twigs pop against the saturated sky. She tried to take everything in before darkness fell.

Soko handed Patty starlight scope goggles and showed her how to use them before adjusting them to her head. The gear was large and heavy and pinched her nose. Insects buzzed around, as if they had been waiting for dusk to taunt her. In the dying moments of the sun's glow, light gleamed off the metal wire between Soko's hands. He was holding wooden handles. With sudden speed, he twisted his wrists and then straightened them out. A garotte. He was warming up for the kill. Red washed the sky. Then blackness.

David came over. "Watch your back. Shylock won't forget a beatin'."

"Roger that," Soko answered, watching as David walked away.

Patty adjusted her goggles to better see his face. "Do you think Shylock will come after you?"

"Probably. But with most guys, it's business first. I shouldn't have to worry about him until after he's done this job."

"If he came after me because of a slap, I can't imagine what he'll do to you."

"Guys like him are humiliated by a woman's slap. Challenges their manhood. You've got gumption. I'll give you that. Few people stand up for what they believe in. I like that about you."

# Chapter 14

Our girls, my loves, come once a week to drop off empty boxes for me to fill. Another nursing home brochure shows up with each visit. They talk about downsizing. Clearing the clutter. Using words like hoarding. I've seen those TV shows. I'm not like them.

No one asks me what *I want*. They arrange my life. Not behind my back, but right in front of me. As if they're entitled to make my decisions for me. Like what I want doesn't matter. I've told them I won't go. I know they're worried about me. Wanting the best for me. But they don't know me. Not even my name. What I've been through. What I've seen. I'm just Mom.

My life is divided into piles—keep, toss, or donate. *The Pentagon Papers*, a treasured book, has been thrown into the donate pile. She hears my catch of breath. Like a whimpering pup. What happened in that book changed my life.

"You don't need it," my daughter says. "See how dog-eared it is."

Precisely, because of how many times I've read it. "I want to pass it on to you."

Her hands are rifling through more stuff. "I'm not into those kinds of books."

With my granddaughter's return from university, and with company for dinner, her life is a whirlwind with never enough time. She hardly has time to fit me in.

When she was younger, I didn't burden her with what we had gone through in Vietnam. In her teenage years, she wasn't interested in politics and war. Then off to college. Hardly seeing her. This conversation required more time than she could spend after marriage and the kids. When we were together, I wanted happy memories for all of us without dredging up a disturbing past. But over the years, I wrote it all in my journal.

"Really," my daughter said, seeing me palm the book out of the donate pile. While I flutter the pages, she focused on her watch.

"I have to go. So much to do before dinner. Same time next week?"

I nod, but she's out the door without acknowledging it.

The book, with its bent binding, automatically opens at my usual spot. *The Pentagon Papers* were released in 1971. It was a history of the United States' political and military involvement in Vietnam from 1945 to 1967. The study, by Daniel Ellsberg, contained seven thousand pages of brilliance, stupidity, lies, and secrets. *The Pentagon Papers* were headline news covered in magazines, newspapers, and many books throughout the years.

I read those two highlighted lines. The government sent the warning out to I and II Corp. But by the time they sent the warning out to III Corp, it was too late to be effective. It sounds like, "Oops, so sorry—too late." So sorry, Christopher was killed, and my life was changed forever.

Christopher came home in a body bag, and I couldn't be there. It was too dangerous. Starting my new life in Canada with Soko, I couldn't laugh without feeling guilty. Why should I be happy when Christopher was dead? His beloved song or saying could trigger my sorrow. If Christopher had done what he wanted and became a draft dodger, we'd be here together. I tried not to blame my dad but it was hard. Grief sat like a lump, caught in my throat that couldn't be swallowed. Time never healed that pain.

I turned the pages, stopping at another highlighted part about the butcher's bill—the list of dead soldiers. Who could think this title appropriate? Writing names like a long grocery list of human carcasses.

The cost of doing business. And Christoher, another slab to add to their invoice. Heartless. That's all he was to them. He died for the politicians and general's lies and stupidity, and they didn't give a shit.

Generals play their big-boy war games while soldiers blindly follow orders, used like green plastic toys—with no feelings or flesh. And for what? Because generals are tired of being on the sidelines waiting to be tagged in. They barter for war to prove themselves. Stroking their egos with the rising numbers killed.

I've seen pictures from 1968 of them sitting in the West Wing of the White House. The room was a bowling alley built for President Truman in 1947 before President Kennedy had it converted into a situation room.

It hadn't lost its original game room intent. President Johnson loved to ride in helicopters. He had big-boy toys. Sitting in his custom-made green vinyl helicopter chair, he orchestrated the play. The Secretary of Defense pushed a toy flag into a city name on the map of Vietnam framed like a sandbox sitting on the table. Generals moved tiny tanks around cities and provinces with their strategies.

The book. All these pages. My thumb slid along the outside edges, making them turn quickly into a blur, fanning my face. I didn't have to read the highlighted sections. I knew what was in them.

Over and over again, the strategy for the Tet Offensive was detailed and explained through captured enemy documents. Everything from what, when, where, why, and how. Ignored! What more could the politicians and generals have asked for? They had all the answers months before the Tet Offensive started. It was spelled out in the captured enemy directives. And still, they didn't feel the need to warn commanders in the field to protect their soldiers! Why? Why wait until it's too late to cancel the ceasefire?

*The Pentagon Papers* answered all my questions. The truth was quoted in these reports that Ellsberg gathered.

WHAT: A report titled Enemy Infiltration concluded that a major offensive was coming. The Viet Cong were converging on the cities. It was generated by the army operations center in the Long Binh Post in Saigon from intelligence analysis in USRV. It was sent with a note attached by Military Assistance Command in Vietnam. It talked about the author and clarified that this was written by a woman, who was black and had only been in-country for three months. Everything about the author, but no comment on her findings. In other words, they were told to ignore it.

Women weren't listened to. She had the trifecta, woman, black and rookie, going against her. If they had just investigated her claims, Christopher might be alive. Hopefully, after all these decades, men's attitudes have changed and my girls are taken seriously at work.

It wasn't until January 29, 1968, that the generals listened. According to the Pentagon Papers, The South Vietnamese raided a house and captured eleven Viet Cong agents. They found a tape recorder and two tapes. The Viet Cong had planned to capture a local radio station and broadcast their propaganda. The North Vietnamese were going to take over major cities, government, and military installations and encouraged a general uprising. They were trying to convince the South Vietnamese that the Americans were their common enemy, and request their support. Because they just wanted peace for their country as a whole. But there was that telling threat at the end—join or they would be considered traitors.

Lieutenant Colonel Pham Minh Tho played the tapes over the phone for the Joint General Staff in Saigon. The warning was sent to I and II Corp. It was too late when III Corp got it because most men were out partying for the Tet New Year.

WHEN: It was headline news. In the January 1st, front page edition of the Party newspaper, Nhan Dan, it read: **Onward to Final Victory-Uncle Ho's combat order.**

*It is titled: Command to Advance and Call to Charge.*

*This spring far outshines the previous springs,*
*Of victories throughout the land come happy tidings.*
*Let the South and North emulate each other in fighting the US*
aggressor!
*Forward! Total victory shall be ours.*

The Defense Department had a copy of this news clip along with another captured document that predicts the Viet Cong revolution will succeed by mid-1968 and that the civilians should expect their Viet Cong and North Vietnamese family members home around the 5th of August 1968.

WHERE: Since October 1967, the Defense Department had sat on this captured document. The final phase of the revolution is within reach. Attack major towns and cities including Saigon. Use strong military attacks in coordination with the uprising of the local population and liberate the capital city of Saigon. Allies should rally enemy brigades and regiments to their side and spread our propaganda.

*And still, the politicians did nothing.*

WHY: More proof was in the Joint Chief's archives and dated the 5th of January 1968. It determined the time is ripe for the implementation of a general uprising to take over power in South Vietnam. The masses are ready for action. The reasons: deteriorating morale in the U.S.A., the conflict between the Americans and the puppet authority-South Vietnamese government leaders, and friction between the Doves and Hawks.

HOW: Three thousand Communist soldiers concealed machine guns and bazookas entering the cities on buses, taxis, motor scooters, bicycles or just walking, and this black woman rookie was the only one who noticed and reported it.

*How could these politicians and generals ignore her observations?*
They had captured directives that backed her up like this one.

Use very strong military attacks in coordination with the uprising of the local population to take over towns and cities. Troops should flood the lowlands. They should move toward liberating the capital city Saigon, take power, and try to rally enemy brigades and regiments to our side one by one. Propaganda should be widely disseminated among the population in general and leaflets should be used to reach enemy officers and enlisted personnel. The above subject should be fully understood by cadre and troops; however, our brothers should not say that this order comes from the Party and Uncle (Ho Chi Minh, the Communist leader of North Vietnam), but to say it comes from the liberation front. Also, do not specify times for implementation.

*How could so many documents be disregarded? Such stupidity cost too many lives.* I clap the book closed. I love it for its honesty but am disgusted by it.

My dad used to say, "Time will tell." I learned through the decades, that truth comes in drips. It started with *The Pentagon Papers.* Fifty years later, after the people involved had died and interest waned concerning Vietnam, classified documents were tacitly declassified.

Secrets. It all came down to secrets. Covering up despicable deeds. Hiding evidence or stupidity by classifying it. Like me, Soko was obsessed with uncovering the truth. He told me that commanders in the field were largely promoted based on high body counts. Some commanders took advantage of free-fire zones to get their numbers up. And field units had body count competitions. All in the name of promotions. It didn't matter if they were civilians. It was a body count. So, I wasn't surprised when I read about that. My dad's prized saying was: "If you don't want people to know what you did, then you shouldn't have done it."

My fingers caressed the rippled cover of the October 2018 issue of Defining the Times Magazine. Champagne bubbles had splashed it when the waiter popped the cork. We were all gussied up for that occasion. Soko looked dapper. It's hard to believe he died a month later. Heart attacks are difficult to predict. I'm grateful we had that special time. This outing was five-star, from the restaurant to the conversations about generals with the same rank. We were celebrating the latest document that had been declassified. It was headline news. There were pictures of the cable from General Westmoreland to Admiral Sharp in Hawaii plastered in magazines, newspapers, and on the internet. I just had to google it. And there it was. The cable read:

REFERENCE ...FEB 68 FRACTURE JAW

OPLAN FRACTURE JAW HAS BEEN APPROVED BY ME. PUBLICATION IS NOW IN

PROGRESS AND PLAN WILL BE DISPATCHED BY ARMED FORCES COURIER

SERVICES 11 FEB.

ETA HONOLULU ARMED FORCES COURIER STATION 11 1200W FEB.

Many articles informed the public that this cable's reference to "Fracture Jaw" was an operation intended to move nuclear weapons into South Vietnam to use against North Vietnam. This cable dated Feb 10, 1968, sent by General Westmoreland was to start that process.

Another declassified document revealed Westmoreland was planning secret meetings in Okinawa to set this plan into action. He did it all without the knowledge or consent of the president. When the president found out about it, he immediately shut down Operation Fracture Jaw.

Wow, fifty years later, the reason for Soko's mission was finally coming to light. The truth was getting closer to our story. We had been conspirators that night at the five-star restaurant, sharing our theories on who planned the captain's mission. We knew the why. It was because Operation Fracture Jaw was nixed. But why wasn't Westmoreland punished? By classifying this document, the government protected Westmoreland's disloyalty to President Johnson by going behind his back to authorize what the president would not. And why was everyone so naive to believe this treachery would end there? The politicians had no idea the perseverance they were up against. To these schemers, it just meant they had to come up with a new strategy. Soko said that night at dinner, the captain met the men from Washington at a safehouse where their Task Force Red Dragon got the go ahead on Feb 11, 1968. Whoever these schemers were, they didn't take long to react to the president shutting down Operation Fracture Jaw.

***

In the White House on Feb 10, 1968, a political line had been drawn, and within those two factions, strategies and counter-strategies were planned. Dissension ran thick. Democracy was shrouded in webs of deceit with men loyal only to their agendas.

When night had fallen, a meeting of similar topics to the ones discussed at the White House that day continued, but with less formality. Plan B was set into motion on Feb 11, 1968.

After the four bureaucrats had parked their old, rusted cars in front of a ramshackle safehouse in the Deanwood area of Washington, they walked up the stairs, rattling the wrought iron rail with their weight.

It was a neighborhood filled with gangs and violence. Because black residents knew messing with a white person brought police and trouble, it was a safe place for the bureaucrats. They were skulking figures dressed in well-worn overcoats with fedoras pulled down. For tonight, they had left their Mercedes Benzes parked at the mansions of their multi-car garage homes.

One bureaucrat heard something dripping and glanced up to see a row of long icicles along the roof line. Below where they hung, round holes had been made in the snow. They were greeted by an old well-muscled, black soldier who had been born into this block.

"Roof needs to be fixed," one bureaucrat pointed to the rotten wooden porch exposed by the melted snow. "Someone's going to go through."

The soldier nodded. "I'll have it tended to."

The outside of the house was shabby, so it would blend with the rest of the neighborhood. The significance of its army-green color wasn't lost on the bureaucrats. The peeling exterior paint had outlasted the manufacturer's ten-year warranty by half of that. Pitted with rust, the house number hung lopsided above the door.

Without waiting for an invitation, the men stomped into the hall, knocking snow and slush off their boots. Inside, the home was surprisingly clean, with white walls and ceilings. The few pieces of furniture were middle-income: a recliner, two armchairs, a table, a radio, and a TV in the living room.

The kitchen accommodated a large Formica table edged in silver banding, a side cupboard, a cabinet, and six chairs covered in red vinyl. The only wall decoration was a calendar. The three bedrooms upstairs were small.

The old soldier slept in the largest room at the top of the stairs. The bedsheets in the other two rooms were almost new since few bodies had touched the softness of their four hundred and eighty thread count. Strong deadbolt locks were on every door and window, but for the soldier, there was no better security than the old, bare, creaky hardwood floors or the wooden staircase that would send out a warning with each step.

Respecting the privacy of his employers, he went upstairs while the bureaucrats continued to the kitchen at the back of the house.

The four men referred to themselves by code names only. They were Mr. Gold, Red, White, and Blue. They knew any place could be easily bugged and conversations recorded, and had arranged this location themselves on many occasions.

The political debates on Feb 10, at the White House were only a formality that prompted their plan. These men had already made crucial decisions about the Russian Chief Marshall of Artillery's fate. They had to stop him from supplying nuclear weapons to North Vietnam. If the USA couldn't have nuclear weapons in Vietnam, the North Vietnamese shouldn't have them either. They knew the Chief Marshall had to die. They knew how many American boys they were saving. They knew they were the real patriots of America.

The conflict between Doves and Hawks created this new faction within the government that kept back-door politics alive. These Hawks weren't about to have their military force surrender at Khe Sanh to this pissant of a country. They wouldn't be subjected to the same fate as the French at the battle of Dien Bien Phu. Their country's superpower status would not be deemed ineffectual. They weren't just fighting the North Vietnamese, they were also fighting their Russian backers. War brings out all adversaries.

For a mission of this critical nature, it was important that each of them knew precisely where the operation was at any given point. After sharing logistical information on the state of their Plan B, the men sat back wrapping up the residual pieces.

"What a fucking debacle today at the White House, huh?" said Mr. Gold seated at the head of the table.

"That seems to be every day now," Mr. White said sitting next to him. "Luckily, we have the gentlemanly planner of assassination on our side. And our assassin."

"Mohammed Tehrani is an efficient operative," Mr. Red echoed Mr. White.

Mr. Blue thumbed through a stack of maps. "We have to hope Mohammed earns his money."

Tapping his cigarette into an ashtray in the middle of the table, Mr. White said, "When will we know what's happening?"

"Since there's no communication allowed until the point of drop off, we won't know if the captain and his men have completed their task until they reach the Saigon embassy. And then it will take twenty-four hours before we can return here for the captain's full debriefing. Until then, we can be assured that our decisions have been for the greater good of our country."

Mr. Blue closed the map that had been spread out on the kitchen table. "This had better work."

Mr. White took note of the men around him. "It's our only option since the President shut down Operation Fracture Jaw."

"Yeah, fucking bullshit luck. Everything was in place. Westy authorized it. Those nukes would have solved our problem." Mr. Red collected the maps from the table and stored them in the side cupboard. "I've got my suspicions on who warned LBJ about that 'top-secret' cable."

Mr. Gold waved his hands. "We were so goddamned reasonable. Suggesting bombing North Vietnamese dikes and locks to flood the farmland and create famine, sinking Soviet ships bringing in arms, invading Laos and Cambodia, increasing the bombing efforts, and using nuclear weapons. So, what else can you do when you're continuously shut down."

"That's McNamara and his 'Wiz Kids' for you," Mr. Red said. "They don't care about our unanimous consensus. If they had listened to us and did what we told them, this war would already be won. But oh no, they want their dog and pony show, afraid of alienating world opinion and creating more unrest and protests."

Mr. Blue butted out his cigarette in the ashtray. "They don't understand, Tet is a complicated strategy. And a strategy of this magnitude and genius relies on a Plan B. Giap has been quoted as saying, there is no such thing as a single strategy. He believes in simultaneous military, political and diplomatic strategies with multiple objectives."

"How can you reason with idiots who think that when all-important North Vietnamese diplomats disappear from their posts for a month, it's a bid for peace! And how about when Giap disappeared from Hanoi, even missing the twenty-third anniversary party on December 22 of the founding of his army? White House morons couldn't see that was suspicious." All heads nodded at Mr. White.

Mr. Blue pushed the ashtray aside. "I got tired of the duty officers reading the daily cables. Ten days of artillery bombardment at Khe Sanh. Then suddenly, not one shot was fired on the day of Tet and for the next two days."

Mr. Red got up and brought back four glasses setting them on the table. He nodded toward Mr. Blue. "And when you asked why Giap put those forty thousand North Vietnamese at Khe Sanh and didn't use them when all hell broke loose, no one paid attention. Alarms should have been going off. Instead, the politicians think it's okay to leave Khe Sanh exposed when we have nuclear weapons to defend it."

Without having to walk anywhere, Mr. Gold reached into a cabinet nearby and pulled out a bottle of whiskey. "I tried to tell them Giap was holding them in reserve for his Plan B."

Mr. Blue received the first shot. "Everyone was too busy reacting to all those other attacks."

The slam of the bottle hitting the table emphasized Mr. Gold's words. "Well, we're shutting down Giap's grander scheme now. And he just opened the door, or should I say a window of opportunity by positioning those forty thousand troops around Khe Sanh. Leaving the border unprotected. It let our Task Force slip right past them."

"Good thing we had our eyes on them?" Mr. Red watched as a full shot glass was set in front of him.

"And with our bombers confirming that Task Force Red Dragon crossed the DMZ at the anticipated time, everything is going as planned," Mr. Gold said.

Glasses were clicked when Mr. White said, "Let's hope the Task Force slays our Red Dragon."

"According to the latest surveillance I shared with you, the Russian Chief Marshall of Artillery has been at Giap's headquarters for two days now. They must be gathering the results of Tet and analyzing them, just as we are."

"We've got Giap where we want him. For all his planning we're one step ahead of him," Mr. Red sighed after chugging the shot. "LBJ may have taken away our nuclear weapons but we're going to make sure Giap can't get nukes from Russia."

His shot glass in hand, tapping it against the table, Mr. White said, "I thought for sure when that captured Russian document was read about the high financial toll this war is taking on their country, they would see we were right."

"They can't read between the lines." Mr. Gold filled his glass.

Mr. White took a sip. "Yeah, and them accusing you of creating lines."

"I'm not creating the words when they are right there in black and white in front of them. Why should our guys in the field risk their lives to get this information when we won't react to these captured documents? That Russian document spelled it out for them, 'When all else fails, we must use the ultimate weapon to ensure a speedy end to this war or financial ruin will be the result.'"

"I don't know what it would take to make them understand when all else fails refers to the Tet Offensive and it's going to fail and the ultimate weapon is nuclear." Mr. Blue lit another cigarette.

Mr. Gold nodded in agreement. "Politicians don't act, they debate. They would have gone on debating while Russia supplied nuclear weapons to the North and we would have ended up losing this war."

"We're the ones protecting the country. Unlike us, Washington won't assume anything." Smoke rings curled around Mr. White's words. "Do you think the Russians found out about Westy's plan to move the nukes?"

"Who knows?" Mr. Gold refilled everyone's glass. "Here's to a successful mission."

They clicked their glasses together and gulped down their drinks. The meeting was concluded, and the four men left the house one at a time. After the last man was out, the old soldier came downstairs and bolted the door.

# Chapter 15

The men crowded around the captain in their usual teams of two as if the sun going down was a signal. Patty, teamed with Soko, watched as the captain stabbed his knife into the ground. His hand worked in a circular motion loosening the dirt around the blade. He pulled the knife out of the ground and poured water into the hollow. It became a miniature mud hole. The men took turns smearing their faces and hands to camouflage the whiteness of their skin.

When it was her turn Soko said, "Don't forget your legs."

Attaching the silencer to his pistol, he said, "The N. V. use tiny lamps made from perfume bottles. Watch for them."

With goggles down, they were on the move. The men had been ordered to protect Shylock. Patty stayed close to Soko. His back was rigid but his arms and legs advanced in fluid movement. He touched her shoulder and held his hand up for stop. Then, he left. A short time later, Patty could see a tiny firefly flicker of light through the trees. She watched as the light fell to the ground and she understood.

Her hand flew to her neck. She knew the thin wire sliced into throats, severed nerves, and cut off cries of alarm. Hearing the trampling of leaves close by, she turned and saw Soko standing beside her in the dark.

The color drained from her face when Soko pointed in the direction he wanted them to go. Blood dripped down his arm. They darted behind trees and bushes, moving in on their prey. She found herself watching for those shafts of light. All the men were accounted for as they converged at the edge of the woods and huddled together.

Using hand signals, the captain instructed the men. Soko took Patty's hand, crouched low to the ground, and stopped behind a large tree in front of a barbed wire barrier. Holding his finger to his lips, he put his hand on her shoulder and pressed her down to sit on the ground behind the tree. He jerked his finger to the ground ordering her to stay put, grabbed her Colt .45 revolver from its pouch and handed it to her.

The captain and the men ducked through the hole in the wire that Soko had cut. Before going through the wire, David unsheathed his dagger and handed it to Patty. Snatching the gun Soko gave her, David shook his head to say "no," before handing it back. She understood. No shots should be heard.

\*\*\*

Armed with explosives, detonators, and his M60 machine gun, Soko crept around equipment and trees to the barracks. Beyond the barbed wire boundary was a large fortress with wide formal stairs leading to French double-doors. Ornate pillars flanked the entrance.

The hundred-year-old plantation was left over from the French conquest of Vietnam during Napoleon III's reign. From the late 1800s to 1954, Vietnam was part of a French colony called Indochina.

A semi-circular balcony jutted out from the front of the third floor. Squat hand-carved rails edged the balcony. It appeared opulent and peaceful until a closer examination exposed it for what it was. No velvet curtains adorned the windows of this falsely picturesque building. A machine gun perched on the balcony. Steel bars sealed lower-level windows. It was unlike any other military installation. There were no army vehicles, only old dilapidated trucks with new engines and good tires.

From the skies, the building would be similar to a palatial estate left over from the French occupation. In keeping with the disguise, the soldiers guarding the fortress were dressed in peasant clothes, but they were heavily armed as they patrolled the area. All the buildings had been painted dull grey so they would easily fade into the mountain.

\*\*\*

Patty's goggles pinched her nose when she leaned her face against the side of the tree hoping to cool her flushed cheeks. She slipped the goggles over her head to take the pressure off. A breaking twig caused her to peek around the tree. She stared straight into a small flickering light.

Shining his light up and down her length, Patty saw the surprised scrutiny on the man's face. She wondered if he'd ever seen a white woman before. Then she thought of the twenty-five-thousand dollar reward. And the torture.

He was a young man, younger than herself. His short-cropped black hair accentuated his thin face and high cheekbones. His body was lean and lacked the brawn she associated with strength. He was pleasant looking until a smile revealed stumps of decayed teeth. Reaching down, he gently patted her hand. His touch reminded her of the soft stroke from the little girl's mother. But she couldn't be fooled. It was always about money. He might be nice, but the people he handed her over to would be monsters.

She clasped the dagger handle in the hand that was hidden under her leg. Deliberately, she waited and let him think she was hurt and needed help to get up. When he knelt in close and clasped her elbow to coax her up, Patty thrust the knife into him. The blade hit bone. Using her body weight, she forced herself to push harder. The blade slid off the bone and sank into his flesh. It was easier to push, but harder to make herself do it. Clutching the hilt of the dagger, her knuckles pressed against the roundness of his chest. He was thin more like a child than a man. Her fingers froze against his body. His hand still held the light. Patty could see the shock and pain in his eyes before the perfume bottle fell. She mirrored his expression with her shock at what she had done. The cut in the palm of her hand stung from the pressure.

There was no hate or dislike. Patty wanted to believe that he was evil and that she was the good person. But the dagger was in her hand and his blood was dripping down her arm. He didn't scream. She was the one who quietly cried. Warm and sticky, his blood slithered between her fingers. Patty felt the suction release and heard the gush of air squeezed from his lungs as his body slid back dislodging itself from the dagger she still gripped.

***

David had set explosives in two of the barns that housed the munitions and the gasoline drums and was on his way to the third barn. The miniature homemade lamps the guards used pinpointed their location and made it easier for David to elude them. Many of the cadres were positioned at the back of the plantation where access to the fortress was expected. Scaling the mountain had never been considered an alternate defensive position. Therefore, few sentries were at the front. There was little movement inside the fortress.

Black on black, Soko melted into the night, sneaking from one hiding place to another, setting explosives. Ducking between trucks when he heard voices, he waited until their conversations trailed off into the night. A burst of laughter from inside the barracks was barely audible above the constant drone of a generator that supplied light to the barracks and fortress.

Soko worked swiftly to collect distributor caps from the line of vehicles. Next to the trucks was a large gasoline drum where he found four heavy gas cans. He set explosives beside them before picking up a can with each hand. He poured gasoline from one of the cans that ran from the drum to the line of trucks. The truck closest to the fortress, he left intact. Sneaking back to that truck, he put the other gas can on the passenger floorboards before bending down to pick a reed of grass. With no one in sight, Soko opened the gas tank and used the reed as a dipstick. Luckily, the tank was full.

\*\*\*

General Giap's office was in a private section of the fortress down a hall and around the corner from the third-floor balcony. He and the Russian Chief Marshall of Artillery were once again reviewing the latest statistical reports on the Tet Offensive. They listed the American installations they had attacked, the cities they had besieged, and the overall damage caused to date.

This was Giap's second day in conference with the Russian. After hours of debate, the Russian hadn't taken off his jacket or loosened his tie. Embroidery embellished the lapels and epaulets. A star decorated the tie. Two rows of medals ran across the left side of his jacket with a singular ribbon and star above them. The right side displayed vertical rows of ornate stars.

He tapped his fingers on Giap's desk. "This offensive was to be the end of the war. We have supplied extra food, military armaments, heavy artillery, and equipment to ensure a speedy victory. All these reports can't confirm what we want to hear. The American forces were hard hit, but they are regaining territory."

Giap sat behind his desk. "Ho Chi Minh's predictions were derailed by revenge. With our propaganda, we thought we could sway the South to our side."

"Why would the South fight for your side when your Viet Cong are rounding up and killing important people in the South? You led us to believe you had control over the Viet Cong. These reports contradict all expectations."

With his arm, the Russian brushed aside the reports. "The probability of failure seems inevitable."

Giap's rounded shoulders sagged, the buttoned-down, medal-free, green long-sleeve shirt with red embroidery on the collar, as limp as its wearer. He folded the maps, reports, and paperwork cluttering his desk and tucked them into a secure hiding place. It had already been a long day. The Russian, his back to the door, watched while sipping vodka.

***

It was easier for one man to creep undetected inside the fortress than if the captain and all his men went in. Once Henry was inside a third-floor room, he locked the door. Cutting away a small portion of the plaster wall under the window, he anchored a rope around the wooden stud. Cadres patrolled the front and back entrances of the fortress. This window was on the east side. Henry dropped the rope out the window to the captain and his men on the ground. Camouflaged by the blackness of night and thick vines that covered the exterior wall, they started their ascent. Easily scaling the building, they slipped in through the third-floor window where they were met by Henry.

With precision, they darted down halls, checking rooms, surprising a shocked enemy, and taking him out silently. They left the dead man behind the third-floor machine gun propped up by the wall, blood dripping from his neck. The few cadres inside who patrolled the third floor of the fortress, whom they met along their way were also left dead and hidden from sight.

Turning a corner into a short hall, the muted spit from Shylock's rifle was quick to take out an armed sentry guarding a door. Thudding to the floor, the sentry's black heels scuffed the wood as he was dragged to another room. They had checked every room on this floor except this one. And it was the only one guarded. The captain stood in front of the door and surveyed over his shoulder making sure his men were ready.

Bursting into the room, the spit of gunfire splintered the mahogany desk, with bits of wood sent flying across the room. The wheels on an overturned chair were still spinning when the firing stopped. Two half-full glasses sat opposite each other on the desk. The captain sniffed the Vodka in the glasses. Walking to the other side of the desk, he saw a drop of blood on the trap door underneath it. The captain lifted the hinged door. A chute went down and disappeared into the next floor. Tunnels and escape routes were not uncommon and even predictable. Wherever Giap and the Russian ended up, it was certain they would have a vehicle nearby to make their escape.

The captain had no idea how many vehicles were at the back of the fortress. If Giap left, he would take a large portion of his cadre with him for protection. That would make the odds of escaping for the Americans even greater.

Several shots rang out. The commotion of men below stairs brought the captain and his men running down the hall to the room where their climbing gear was left.

\*\*\*

When the gunfire started, Soko waited a few seconds for the North Vietnamese soldiers to run out of the barracks. Waiting for the soldiers to get closer to the explosives, Soko detonated them. Dirt and men flew in the air, disappearing into a cloud of smoke. Bodies were scattered throughout the area. Loud blasts in rapid succession ripped apart the old barns. Fires burned in every direction, creating thick grey smog.

\*\*\*

Patty had watched Soko disable the vehicles and check the gas tank in the vehicle near the fortress. She assumed they would take that one. Even though Soko told her to sit tight, she couldn't resist. He was too far away to backtrack. She wouldn't take the chance of them leaving without her. Forcing her clenched fist open, she felt stringy, mucus threads from her palm to her outstretched fingers. Running her hands through the grass, she wiped them clean.

She studied the dead soldier beside her. She hadn't fooled him. Even with her hair pulled back, he knew she was a white woman. But it had saved her. Could she risk running out dressed the way she was? Twenty-five-thousand was a lot. At least, they'd need her alive, so they wouldn't shoot her. She examined his clothes. They'd fit. But running toward Soko and the Americans dressed as the enemy! Soldiers shot at the biggest target, usually at the chest, and they wouldn't be noticing or aiming at her face. Discarding the idea and slipping the dagger into her belt, she set off toward the opening Soko had cut in the barbed wire.

While climbing between the open fencing, an explosion erupted. Flames shot up and bathed Patty in white light. Startled, she let go of the flat piece of wire she was holding to creep through the opening. The wire snapped back and snagged her shorts. In the burst of flames, the light made her an easy target. Her hands worked to yank her shorts free but the blue jean material was too strong to rip. Hands panicked, and were not strong enough. She twisted and turned her body.

Afraid the enemy would spot her or that the wire would wrap around her, she stopped struggling. Taking out the dagger, she sliced the side of her shorts and climbed out to the other side of the fence. She felt the blue jean material flap against the side of her leg as she sprinted, pistol in hand, towards the centre of action.

Choking on the smoke, she knelt to watch the commotion and chaos. Singed, bristles of nose hair tingled and made her feel like she was snorting fire. Men were running, blasting weapons; buildings were ablaze and explosions were all around.

Patty noticed the lone figure dressed in black. She headed in his direction. In a sudden blast of brilliant light, she saw Shylock. She had a bead on his rifle barrel as it trailed Soko, giving her an excuse. Without hesitating, she fired repeatedly until Shylock fell to the ground.

\*\*\*

Soko turned at the sound, and saw Patty racing toward him, and ran in her direction. Passing Shylock's body, he put a bullet in his head. Another explosion pelted dirt and debris in their direction. Batting at the smoke that shifted with the breeze, he called out her name. She grabbed his arm.

"He was aiming at me, wasn't he?"

"Yes." The word gasped out of her.

He clutched her hand. "Thanks."

They rushed over to the vehicle he hadn't stripped. He opened the passenger door for her.

"Stay down."

Darting around to the driver's door, he climbed in and hot-wired the truck. The captain and his men were outside returning fire. Soko detonated the gasoline drums. The explosion ignited the row of trucks, simulating a giant string of firecrackers going off. Gasoline fumes sprayed into the air, licked by the fire and combusted into flame throwers.

Soko had created a thick smoke screen for David as he dodged behind obstacles and made his way over to the truck. Gripping his M60 machine gun, Soko ran to the back of the truck, dropped the tailgate, and flipped back the canvas wall. Bracing his weapon against his hip, he spread his legs for balance.

The heat from the five hundred and fifty, high-velocity bullets he fired made his forehead sweat. The heavy cartridge belt danced against his chest. David slid over to the truck's rear end and joined him. Together, they provided the firepower to cover the rest of their men as they jumped into the back of the truck.

Henry's feet dragged the ground while the men on either side of him ran to the back of the truck. Dumped into the truck, his two rescuers leaped in beside him. The captain, in mid-stride, shouted, "Let's go," before propelling himself into the back of the truck.

Dashing around to the front of the truck, Soko jumped in and slammed the door shut. The men in the back pulled up the tailgate and used it to steady their rifles. With the M60, David provided the firepower that kept the enemy hidden from sight as they exited around the back of the fortress to the road.

"Take off your goggles," Soko said as he threw his on the seat. "The light will hurt your eyes."

Patty threw them off in a panic. They hit the gasoline can at her feet.

The truck lurched forward at a reckless speed, guided by its headlights down a dirt road engulfed in darkness. Shifting gears, the engine roared as Soko maneuvered the vehicle through dangerous turns and curves.

Soko's careful study of the maps in advance of their mission meant he knew the quickest and safest route to reach their landing zone. With expert maneuvering, he negotiated each hairpin turn.

"Two trucks gaining from behind," roared the captain from the window flap near Soko's head. The blooper was set up with two men manning the M79 grenade launcher. Its plinking sound was drowned out by the other weapons. Patty jumped at the first explosion and slumped down to the truck's floorboards knocking the gas can over. She stood it upright again.

David cut a large opening in the side of the canvas near the cab of the truck. Catching a glimpse from Patty's side-view mirror, of the flapping canvas, Soko yelled at Patty, "Get up."

She didn't seem to understand but obeyed.

"Roll down your window."

When she leaned out the window to see what was happening, he snapped, "Get your head in. That's what mirrors are for."

After several tries, the grenade launcher used by the men in the back of their truck finally hit its mark and exploded under the right front tire of the approaching truck. The force flipped the pursuing truck over on its side. The wheels were still spinning when another explosion ignited a fire. Flames chewed the canvas sides of the enemy truck and devoured it.

The blaze from the truck lit up the night, illuminating their truck's metal running board. David, hanging off the side of the truck, moved his foot off the wood slat to the running board securing both his feet. The captain passed a bazooka out to him. Patty watched from the side-view mirror as David inched along until he was in front of her window.

"Get ready," he bellowed over the steady din of gunfire and shoved the bazooka through the open window to Patty.

Patty was familiar with the black cylinder rocket launcher and knew it needed open spaces to be fired to accommodate the blast from behind. It was useless in the back of the truck. Soko watched as she unsnapped the little shoulder mount and put the cylinder on her shoulder. David clutched the roof rack and boosted himself up onto his knees. His knees were replaced by his black dusty boots that rested on the window sill.

"Get ready to hand it up," Soko said.

Patty turned her head when an explosion ripped into the road and sprayed dirt and stones into her hair. In one swift movement, she watched David push off and he disappeared overhead. Then his arms dangled over the edge of the roof with fingers flapping impatiently.

Patty knelt on the seat and hefted the bazooka out of the window into David's hands that disappeared overhead onto the roof with the weapon.

The second vehicle, a heavy armor-plated truck swerved just in time to avoid a fiery collision with their first truck. The action was so sudden and forceful that men inside the second vehicle were thrown into the air and collided with each other. In her side mirror, Patty saw weapons dropped in a haphazard disarray and the melee of bodies trying to right themselves only to produce further chaos.

This was David's best chance. Soko kept the truck steady. Luckily, they were on a straightaway. Then David fired. The second truck blew up with a tremendous loud sharp bang propelling parts and men through the air. Another explosion inside the truck sent up a white spotlight of intense heat that layered colors like a gasoline rainbow on pavement.

David slid off the roof, feet first, through the window frame and landed on Patty's lap.

He laughed and got up so she could slide out from underneath him.

For two hours, the truck, like the road lines on the map, progressively marked their route until they reached their destination. Soko stopped the vehicle under a canopy of teak and mahogany trees. They were on the other side of the demilitarized zone, back in South Vietnam.

"We have three hours," the captain said. "Start clearing the LZ."

\*\*\*

The flare to signal the chopper would also signal their position to the enemy and attract hostile fire. The wait was unnerving. Defensive positions were assumed within the demarcation. The men stood in the black void of night and listened.

If time were measured by thoughts, Patty was certain an eternity had gone by. Mentally, she listed all the reasons why the chopper wouldn't come. It had been shot down, had engine trouble, run out of gas, or couldn't find them …. She was afraid to hope.

"Still have my knife?" David's words startled her. She took it out of her belt and handed it to him.

He touched the thick blade feeling the stickiness that ran its length to the hilt. "Y'all used this?"

"Yeah."

He pulled his goggles down and gaped at her shirt. "When we was in the truck, I'd seen a big stain on yur shirt, but I'd thought it was dirt." He turned the blade over and examined it.

"Bled like a stuck pig. Put yur weight into it to bury the knife to the hilt. Not easy to do. No escapin that feelin. He's part of y'all now." He shook his head. "No band-aid cure."

He wiped the blade on his shirt with two strokes on each side, the same motion as sharpening it.

"Killin a man up close is a hard thin' to live with. Y'all have fuckin guts lady."

Patty stared into his goggles before dropping her gaze. *Fucking guts! Is that what it takes? Fucking guts dripping in my lap. Knuckles pushing on hard bone. The lantern – forcing me to see. No hatred, just dark eyes watering, his and mine.*

"Y'all can be on my team any day."

Patty stared up at him. She didn't know how an anti-war protestor should handle praise for killing.

David clapped her on the back like he would one of the guys and said, "Good job."

She watched as he wiped the blade again before putting it back in its sheath.

After clearing a landing zone with the other men, Soko stood beside Patty. "You know how to handle a bazooka, don't you?"

"Yeah. And I knew it was going to take that to penetrate the tank's armor."

"Were you in the army?"

"No. I was born into the army. My dad is a general. By the time I was fifteen, I could shoot targets with the best of them. I loved heavy artillery. Dad called me his little sharpshooter. Even nicknamed me 'Bullseye.'"

"Who's your dad?"

"General Brian Fielding." She picked at the dried blood between her fingers.

"Where's he out of?"

"Fort Benning."

The captain came up beside them. "Her being with us—that's on you. You're going to be explaining that. I'm not getting my ass reamed over this. Washington doesn't like complications."

Patty heard the churning chopper blades but wasn't sure where it was coming from. Soko scanned the treetop level. "See, there it is," he pointed it out.

The noise became progressively louder and matched the heady excitement bubbling inside her. Everyone rubbernecked overhead, uncertain how close it was to them. The aluminum and plexiglass body was illuminated by their red flare.

"It's an INFANT." Patty was reassured by the excitement in Soko's voice.

"We don't need a second flare," the captain said stopping his man from setting off another one. "They'll spot us with the firefly."

The huge high-powered spotlight attached to the Huey lit up the landing zone. Dirt sandblasted the chopper as it set down. Soko took Patty's hand and bounded toward it heedless of the dirt it sprayed into their faces. The force of the rotor's blast pushed against Patty's knees. She leaned her body into the gale-like wind, covering her arm across her face, and squinted against the flying debris. Soko boosted her up into the chopper and David pulled her in.

He took his helmet off, put it on the floor, and sat her on it. "So y'all don't get shrapnel up your ass."

The rest of the men piled in. As the chopper lifted off, the enemy below kept firing at them. The spotlight easily pinpointed their location. Their guns were quieted as rockets blasted from the Huey and the door gunner fired his Gatling gun. Once out of range and seemingly safe, Patty cried long and hard. She'd almost given up on getting home. It was over.

# Chapter 16

Through the years, I'd checked out classified government documents that had been declassified. But, I couldn't believe what I found on the internet. A book reviewed by the New York Times. It was called, *The Declassification Engine by Matthew Connelly, published by Pantheon Books in New York and released Feb 14, 2023*. My computer skills have greatly improved, and I ordered the e-book.

It revealed astonishing information and the attitudes of the times. I turned to the index and started reading the sections about Vietnam.

In the book it outlined how divided the USA was against itself, with generals against government. It posited that in order to de-escalate a crisis it was important to convince one's populace that the enemy was ready to use nuclear weapons. I realized that even today, with the crisis going on in the Ukraine and the one that ended disastrously in Iraq, it was the threat of these weapons of mass destruction that had precipitated action.

I looked at my cherished photo of Soko. I wish you were alive, my love, to read this. So much to talk about and no one to speak with. You told me the men who planned and organized the captain's mission had wanted to nuke North Vietnam. Your words were validated finally. And now others will know! The name that was redacted could have been one of the men I met in that dilapidated house.

My dad and Soko thought his mission hadn't been sanctioned by the politicians. And now, to learn about back-stabbing and cover-ups between politicians and the military in this book, they were probably right.

I wonder if I'd be alive when the government declassifies Soko's mission. Or maybe it was so secret the military kept no records of it. And me, so naive to believe it was over when I was rescued—that was when the real game was just beginning.

\*\*\*

The men squatted shoulder to shoulder leaning out from the chopper as it hovered over Saigon. It was easy to spot the white, concrete, six-storey US Embassy complex surrounded by a ten-foot wall. They landed on the rooftop helipad. After the six-and-a-half-hour battle that had raged through the embassy, the USA was taking no chances. The embassy was no longer interested in showing their good faith in the South Vietnamese's ability to protect their grounds. Instead, they brought in their own troops.

A hole in the concrete wall made by an antitank gun had put an end to the architect's claim that "Bunker's Bunker" was impenetrable. His reputation was gone, confirmed by a gaping hole. Heavily armed troops guarded the workmen as they repaired the damage. An American show of strength was flaunted in the complex and on the rooftop.

Clean-shaven, sweet-smelling US military guards surrounded the chopper when it landed. The guards acted as escorts and shields. If the guards had been startled to see a shapely bare leg hanging from the Huey's door, they didn't let on. It wasn't until David stepped out to reveal his hairy legs in boxer shorts that a few snickers erupted.

Before the chopper landed, David had handed Patty his pants and belt. "To hold up them britches," he said.

Forgetting about her torn shorts, she'd been taken aback when he offered his pants to her.

"Don't want them to see clear to the promised land," he said.

It was funny to hear the other men sing the strip tease song and shout cat-calls as he took them off. Patty held the side of the metal door frame to step out and felt David's hand support her elbow. Can it get any weirder than this? she thought, as guards came alongside her with a stretcher. The captain and Soko helped Henry to the stretcher.

When the rest of the men disembarked, they were herded to the stairwell. The group made their way down six floors to the basement. Along the hallway, sentries guarded entrances throughout the restricted area. A guard knocked on a solid double door with an engraved brass plate that boasted Command Centre.

Little more than salutes were exchanged between the captain and the lieutenant who opened the door.

"Wait here." the captain said, to his men, as the lieutenant escorted him to a colonel, seated behind a desk.

The captain saluted. "I've been advised by Washington that you'll be the facilitator. My men need a shower, fresh clothes, food, and medical attention for minor injuries. I have a woman who needs the same. One man was taken off by stretcher. I'm hoping your doctor can get him ready for transport home with us."

"We can attend to your needs. Lieutenant, please escort our visitors to the showers, round up clean clothes, and see they are fed," the Colonel ordered.

Once outside the colonel's office, the lieutenant pulled out his notepad and pen and recorded the uniform sizes he would need, and then escorted the group down the hall. Patty was the last person to be dropped off at a private bathroom with a shower.

Taking off her shorts, Patty felt something in the back pocket and took it out. She'd forgotten about the photograph Peter had given her. She had to pull on the seal to get it open. Other than being a little bent, it was in surprisingly good shape.

Stepping into the shower, Patty turned the water on as hot as she could stand. The pressure was strong and pummeled her body like a welcomed massage. She winced in pain when the water hit her face and she was quick to turn her back on it. Scrubbing her hair, she felt scabs and bumpy insect bites. The palm of her hand had cleared up nicely. Brown water puddled at her feet before going down the drain. It seemed strange to be clean without a mild scent. The soap and shampoo weren't perfumed, nor the deodorant. Wrapped in a towel, she opened the door to a female staff member who provided her with women's army clothes. She dressed quickly and pocketed the photograph.

They were herded into a private cafeteria area where warming trays were heaped with mashed potatoes, roast beef, corn, and gravy.

The captain waited for Patty to finish her meal and then had her come along with him. He made her wait outside the colonel's door while he went in to speak with him.

The captain returned and called her inside. He placed a paper on the colonel's desk, then shoved her closer to it. "Washington needs as much information as you can give them." Turning to the colonel, he said. "This is their number. When she's done, call them. Say we were on target, but we had an unexpected visitor, and then relay her information."

She wanted to knock that smug veneer off the captain's face. It was like he wanted to show her that he had permission from the highest authority to use the colonel however he chose. Delegating a menial clerical job to the colonel and showing off his power disgusted her.

The colonel addressed Patty. "I'm always happy to speak with a lovely lady."

The colonel took note of the phone number and flipped the paper over. "Who should I ask for?"

"It's a direct line. No names necessary. You just relay the information." The captain saluted and left.

"I'm Colonel Burke. And you are?" He reached out his hand to shake hers.

"Patty Fielding."

He eyeballed her. "I saw your name on an MIA list. Please have a seat." He wrote her name down and asked, "Middle name? Date of birth? Place of birth? Father's first name?" He lifted his pen off the page. "Is that General Brian Fielding by any chance?"

"Yes."

"Of Fort Benning?"

"There and everywhere else."

He smiled. "I served under your father. He helped me a great deal to get through the ranks. He's a well-respected man. How is he doing?"

"I haven't seen him in a while."

"When you see him, please tell him, Colonel Steven Burke sends his regards."

"I will."

"Mother's first and last name?" He continued in a friendlier tone. "Address, social security number? Employer?"

"Why do they need to know all this?"

"Well, it's always good to have this information when we're transporting someone whom we're responsible for."

He concluded the questions, filled in her answers, put the pen down, and took his glasses off. "You have a few hours before boarding, so I suggest you take a nap. It was a privilege to meet the daughter of a man I admire." He shook her hand and called for his lieutenant to escort her to a cot.

Patty accompanied the lieutenant to a drab windowless room lined with cots. She walked to one and unfolded a grey blanket at the end of the bed flicking it over the sheet. Climbing into the crisp coolness, she tucked her feet under the covers. It was great to be in a bed, even if it was just a cot.

Soko shook her awake. Though her stomach was full, and her body clean, she felt worse now than when they first arrived. She was groggy and half asleep. Two hours had been enough time for stiffness and muscle aches to set in.

"It's a good thing we don't have to walk back up those six flights of stairs," he said.

They tailgated the lieutenant and the rest of the men through corridors to a back exit where, a truck, flanked by a military entourage, stood to take them to Tan Son Nhut Airbase. When the back doors opened, Henry was already strapped into a stretcher inside.

"Good to see you," Soko said, hopping into the vehicle.

Henry gazed down at him. "I was talking to a guy who works for Military Assistance Command Vietnam—Studies and Observation Group (MACV-SOG) just east of the airbase. He said it was unusual for us to be re-routed through the embassy with the airport so close."

Soko peered up. "I thought so too. I figured, this way, our helicopter flight wouldn't show up on Tan Son Nhut's log if we landed there."

Henry nodded to him. Bouncing around on the truck's bench, the bumpy road kept Patty awake until they arrived at the busy airbase. Their military entourage got out first and encircled them. The captain and his men didn't rely on this polished and cleaned-up version of the military. They hefted their weapons. The captain told the men to watch for snipers as they scanned the still-devastated area.

Soko glanced at one of their escorts. "How bad was it?"

"Twenty-two killed and eighty-two wounded."

The captain's group boarded the plane without incident. It had been refueled, ready for take-off.

Patty sat on a bench at the side of the plane. Her body was numb from exhaustion. She only wished her mind would succumb to that same state. Moving in tight, Soko wrapped his arm around her back, and let her head fall against his chest. A slight movement nudged Patty awake. She watched as Soko unfolded a blanket, spreading it out on the floor in the middle of the aircraft. She was aware of David's babbling and the men's laughter.

"If I'd a had my dog Five Track at the LZ, those fuckin gooks wouldn't been firin up at us," David said. "Best bloodhound I ever had. Even if thar's a bunch a hounds, I can pick out his trail every time. That fuckin dog is hung like a horse with balls so big they drag the ground." The laughter continued.

Soko bunched up another blanket for her head.

"Now Gorgeous, that's his nickname, was slow to start on account he was always humpin someone's leg…"

Somewhere a hundred miles away, she heard Soko say, "Come on."

He put his hands under her armpits, pulled her down on the blanket, and covered her up. She curled on her side. The laughter carried on.

"You missed your calling. You should have been a stand-up comic," Henry said.

"He's just frothing at the mouth," Soko teased. "Been around those dogs of his too long."

The excitement ebbed and so did David's stories as each man curled up in his own space and fell asleep.

*** 

The aircraft danced a jig, caught up in the whirlwind of turbulence. The co-pilot shifted and leaned out of the seat to check on their passengers. "They're out cold."

He reached for his seatbelt while the pilot expertly maneuvered to a smoother altitude.

"Did you notice how no one back there," he motioned with his head, "snores? Don't you think that's weird?"

"Yeah. I've questioned that myself. They tell me they never go into a deep sleep. It's like their mind is still awake, listening. Like they're hovering on the outer edge of sleep."

"Sounds like bullshit to me."

"That's what I thought, until my wife told me it's like how a new mother trains herself to listen to her baby when she sleeps. I can see what she means. My wife used to sleep like a rock until we had our Jimmy. Now she hears every noise that baby makes at night. I swear, she can hear him breathing through the walls. One night, she—"

"Holy shit. What the Christ was that?" the co-pilot said.

A low scream came from the passenger cabin.

"I *almost* shat," the co-pilot said. "I didn't think anything human could sound like that. Did you ..." He peered over at the pilot. His face was white, and his hands were tucked under crossed arms clutching his sides to stop their trembling.

\*\*\*

Patty's low guttural scream erupted tearing through her insides before it spewed from her throat. The sound had the edge of hot steel. The men jolted awake, fumbling for weapons that weren't there.

Patty's body shook. She stretched her fingers out examining her hands. Soko dropped down next to her.

"It's a nightmare." He wrapped his arm around her. She yanked it away and pummeled his chest with surprisingly vicious blows.

"It's Soko, you're safe." He held both her hands for a while. Gradually, her breathing became normal. "It's Soko," he whispered and let go of her hands.

Clarity brought his face and the situation into focus. Her body was rigid, impossible to cuddle. Patty held her hands away from her body to study them again. Violent tremors ran down her.

"Get it off," Patty screamed.

David said, "She used my knife. Blood was to the hilt."

Soko picked up each hand and wiped them on his shirt.

"It's gone. I got it all. There's nothing there," he said.

He turned the palms of her hands down and straightened her stiff arms and laid them beside her.

She felt the harshness in her face soften.

The euphoric feeling of surviving was only a pinprick in time, overwhelmed by what she had done. Soko gathered her ramrod body to his chest and rocked her back and forth.

"It's alright. You're safe. Everything is fine."

Her body refused to relax. She twitched periodically.

He wiped the sweat from her forehead. "I'm here. I won't leave you."

Patty's small fist unclenched, and her spent body fell back against him.

***

Bright sunlight filled the windows. The last to wake up, Patty hugged the blanket, reassured by and listening to those wonderful morning sounds that confirmed there was no enemy around. The captain stretched both arms above his head, making a loud weight-lifting grunt. David sat up and scratched his hairy chest grunting and farting as he leaned over to put on his boots. It was the price they all had to pay for his full belly.

"Oh God, get out of here." Henry hung his arm over the edge of the cot and pushed David, waving his arm to clear the air.

It elicited a big belly laugh from David who seemed to get the biggest kick out of his farts.

"Something must have crawled up inside you and died," the captain said.

David laughed harder. Careful not to step on Patty's socked feet, he stood.

Patty got up and picked up her blankets when she heard the motion of bodies bending and shifting. The men stood in line, waiting their turn for the bathroom.

"I got to piss so bad I can taste it," David said.

But no one offered him their place in line. Patty sat on the bench waiting for the line to clear.

"Where are we headed?"

"Reagan Airport."

David turned. "Yeah, but the captain gets to go to Disneyland East."

Patty looked to Soko for clarification. "The Pentagon."

With her eyes closed, she listened to the conversations and picked out the speakers. David's hillbilly twang was the easiest to distinguish. She was surprised that he was the comedian among them. It seemed unlikely. He had a steady stream of stories that offered a distraction while they waited. The captain spoke in a lecturing self-righteous tone. And she hadn't noticed Henry's accent before.

"You ready for breakfast?" Soko asked.

At the front of the plane was a galley-style kitchen stocked with dry cereal, pigs in a blanket, fruits, yogurt, milk, juices, and coffee.

"Yeah. Just need to go to the restroom first."

When she returned, Soko handed her a pig in a blanket with orange juice.

"There's lots more of everything," he said. "Help yourself." Patty came back with a plateful and sat beside Soko. The men finished breakfast and opened a pack of cards that was left for them in the kitchen.

"Anyone for straight seven?" David shuffled the cards.

"Where nothing's wild but the dealer," Henry added.

Soko and Patty retreated to a quiet corner.

Cigarette smoke drifted toward them. "Do you mind if I light up?" Soko asked.

"Not if I can have one too."

He tapped one out of his pack and offered it to her. After he lit their cigarettes, she took his lighter and read the inscription. "Morality is a choice." An atonement, she wondered, or a warning of what men were capable of? When she asked him for the answer, he said, "A reminder, so I don't lose who I am over there."

Patty set the cigarette in the ashtray holder as if it was too distracting. "My brother Christopher had written almost those same words in a letter to me. That's what he said could happen—what he was afraid would happen. He didn't want to lose who he was. It was the reason I came to Vietnam. For him. To remind him of home. So, he knew. He wasn't this person the army turned him into."

"I get it. Family is everything. I'd do anything for my sisters. We're close. We get together as often as we can. Dad and I have barbequing contests, and my sisters compete with side dishes and desserts. We have feasts."

"Sounds nice."

"What about your dad? A general, that's pretty impressive."

"We don't get along that well, and my mom died four years ago. So, it's really just my brother and me. What about your dad?"

"He's a civil rights lawyer. Great guy. One of those cuddly bear types."

When Soko got up to use the bathroom, the captain came over to Patty. "Soko's not going to be interested in a whore like you."

"Are you always that gullible, or is it just when you think with your dick? I don't have gonorrhea. I never did. I just told you that to stop you from touching me."

The shock on his face was worth the pain from her bruised cheek when she smiled.

"And I'm still a virgin, thanks to Soko stopping Shylock. Cherry intact." *Okay, so that part was a lie, but I couldn't resist twisting the knife. And what idiot believed there were any twenty-four-year-old virgins left? The sixties screamed sex, drugs, and rock n' roll.*

The captain breathed heavily; his eyes squinted with brows furrowed. His jaw was clenched as tight as a fist. He stalked away.

"You seem happy," Soko said when he resumed his seat beside her.

"I feel like the cat that ate the canary." She put her hand over her mouth to hide her smile.

"Okay, I guess that's a good thing?" Soko raised his eyebrow.

Hours disappeared in conversation. When they were over Washington D.C. airspace, Soko pointed out the area he lived in. The pilot announced their descent, with the trip ending too soon for the two. The plane touched down screeching its tires on the Reagan Airport runway. Safe and home at last.

# Chapter 17

"What now?" Patty asked Soko.

"I imagine you'll be debriefed at the Pentagon. That's where the captain's going. It's a little over a mile from here. When they find out who you are, they'll call your father."

"I'll bet they've already done that, and he's waiting for me."

"How would they know you're with us?"

"Back at the embassy, Colonel Burke asked me all kinds of questions. Turns out he's a good friend of my dad. The captain told him to question me and forward my info to Washington."

"What kind of questions?"

"My name, my parent's name, address, social security number. Stuff like that."

"Why would they need all that?" Soko flicked his cigarette repeatedly. His eyes were going back and forth like he was going through a lot of detail in his head.

"What's wrong?"

"It's a good thing you're a general's daughter. Give me your phone number."

They exchanged contact information. "If you need anything, call me."

Patty checked out the name he'd written. "Thanks, Dennis."

"I'd like to stay in touch."

Patty felt her cheeks blush and knew her freckles would create the impression that they were sliding down a hill. She hated appearing younger than her twenty-four years. She hadn't fallen in love with his features. He was average. It was his personality and character that made him handsome beyond belief. She was thrilled that he wanted to continue seeing her. Scoping out the airplane window, Patty felt Soko's body press against hers. There was no armor truck to transport them, nor soldiers to protect them this time.

"No welcoming committee," Patty said, expecting to see her dad.

"My car is over there," he pointed to a red Mustang.

They heard the rattle outside from the stairs being rolled over to the plane's hatch. The co-pilot stepped out from the cockpit and unlatched the door to the stairs. Crisp air unclogged their sinuses, and the wind bristled their skin. Soko draped a blanket around her shoulders. The group descended the staircase and had only taken a few steps on the tarmac when a black sedan pulled up beside them. The chauffeur got out and instructed Patty to join the captain before he walked back to the vehicle.

Patty tugged Soko's shirt. "Where's my dad?"

"It'll be okay." He tucked his shirttail back into his pants and walked with her.

The chauffeur held the door open.

"Why isn't my dad here?" She asked no one in particular as she climbed into the car next to the captain.

She saw the worry in Soko's eyes. David walked over to Soko and yanked his arm. He wouldn't move. Taking the lighter out of his pocket, he rubbed his thumb over the engraved words. It seemed like a nervous gesture. *Morality is a choice.*

She watched Soko and David walk to their cars parked under a carport.

***

David stopped and waited while Soko lit a cigarette. "Something isn't right about this. No father whose daughter was in 'Nam during the Tet would miss reuniting with her on the tarmac. Especially a military man with clout. Patty's a witness."

Soko blew the smoke away from David's face. "A problem." He fixated on the sedan, giving the evil eye to the captain in the backseat. "When there's no time to fix or solve problems, they're eliminated." The words were said more to himself than to David.

David looked back at the sedan too.

Patty waved back at them. Wondering if their cars would start, Soko held her attention while getting into his car. Smoke belched from the exhaust.

\*\*\*

The chauffeur was held up while the captain stuck his head out the window talking to a soldier he knew. As soon as the captain's window was up, the sedan headed out. Soko had said the airport was a little over a mile from the Pentagon. The driver wasn't going to the Pentagon. They were traveling into the thick of the city in a poor district within short years of a wrecking ball. Garbage and broken beer bottles decorated the streets and sewers. The street they turned into was narrow with graffiti-layered signs only recognizable by their shape. The sedan stopped in front of a house.

"Why are we here?" Patty asked when the chauffeur parked the car.

"This is one of our safehouses." The chauffeur remained seated.

The captain nudged Patty out of the vehicle.

*This can't be right. Soko said we'd go to the Pentagon.* She traipsed behind the captain up the concrete steps, as the rail jiggled in her hand, and stepped onto the newly patched wooden porch. Bubbly pockets of rust blistered a tarnished metal mailbox. The captain rang the doorbell. The old man who answered the door let them in without asking what they wanted. He escorted them to the kitchen. She was reassured by the inside of the house. It was refurbished and clean. Somehow, it made her feel safer.

"Please join us, Miss Fielding," one of the four men inside said, pulling out the chair next to him for her. "I'm Mr. Gold. That's all captain, you can wait in the living room."

The captain and the old man left closing the door behind them.

"I'm sorry about all this cloak and dagger stuff," Mr. Gold said. "I'm afraid introductions have to be limited for security reasons." He introduced the other men, going clockwise around the table. "This is Mr. Blue, Mr. Red, and beside him, Mr. White.

"We had a security breach and thought it prudent to take precautions. We have contacted your father, informing him of your safe return home. Unfortunately, we have to postpone your reunion for a while. Your father was part of a team that was sent to negotiate with Cambodian officials. Since he was over in Vietnam trying to find you, we took advantage of his availability. He must stay and complete the task. We have assured him; we will tend to your safety."

Mr. Red took over. "During the initial attack on the embassy, it was discovered that one of the entrusted Vietnamese employees was, in fact, a spy. And we feel certain there could be spies at home here in the US as well, who will want to know what the captain's mission was about. Although he is not confessing yet, news of your participation in this covert operation could have been leaked. A high-ranking officer from the embassy was killed. We assume they were looking for information. We're not certain his death has anything to do with the captain's mission, but since torture was used, they were trying to find out something."

Mr. Gold put his hand up to silence Mr. Red. "No use scaring her. It might simply be a coincidence. But to be on the safe side, we will delay your release until we find out more."

"Yes," Mr. Red agreed. "You've been through enough. This is just a precaution. No one knew your name so they would have no way of tracking you down."

Patty could feel a knot in her stomach tighten.

Reaching for her hand, Mr. Gold asked, "Are you okay?" His voice was thick with concern. "You look as if you've seen a ghost."

Patty could feel her body trembling. "Who was the man they killed?" Her voice was barely above a whisper.

"His name was Colonel Steven Burke, but I don't know..."

A small moan escaped her lips as she slumped down leaning on the table.

Mr. Gold jumped up and was by her side. "What's wrong? Someone get her some water. Take deep breaths."

Patty gasped, "I told him my name. My father's name. Gave him all my information."

Mr. Gold waved his hand fanning her face. "Why would you have any contact with the colonel?"

"The captain wanted to let someone know I was coming back with them." Her words were puffed out between heavy breaths. Her shaking hand splashed water down the side of the glass that was given to her.

"The captain and his men were on a top-secret mission. We hadn't counted on this. Our men are anonymous. But you ... They can track you down and they use torture." He sank into the chair with a sigh.

*Soko said, that if the North Vietnamese caught her they would torture her.* "You'll protect me, won't you? You have to."

"Of course, we won't desert you now. We must get you someplace safe."

Patty was numb to all that was happening.

Mr. Gold called the captain into the kitchen. The usual self-assured swagger raised his shoulders and made them teeter from side to side as he walked. No one invited him to sit, so he remained standing.

"Captain, do you remember the cabin in the woods that we use for special guests?" Mr. Gold asked.

"I remember the cabin, but not how to get there. It's been a long time."

"We need you to take Miss Fielding there." Mr. Blue flicked through a stack of maps. He pulled one out and opened it up on the table. The captain bent over the map as Mr. Gold traced the route with a red pen.

"It should take about four and a half hours to get there. There's no electricity, but there's a generator on the front porch. There should be firewood piled up there as well. The fridge won't be stocked, so you'll have to take care of that."

"How long will this be for?" Patty addressed Mr. Gold.

"Probably three days."

"What about my dad?"

Mr. White smiled reassuringly. "Not to worry. We'll keep him apprised of the situation. It shouldn't take long to sort this all out."

Mr. Gold pulled a suitcase out from under the table. "When we knew we had to detain you to find out what was happening, we took the liberty of going to your apartment and packing a suitcase. Being a good friend of your father's, I can attest that he would have my hide if I didn't see to your needs properly." He presented her with the suitcase.

Patty smiled, knowing he was right.

"If you don't have any questions or concerns, our man will escort you to a room upstairs where you can rest for a bit before you head out to the cabin."

Patty picked up her suitcase.

"I'm sure you will respect our need for privacy in this matter. Mr. Kline," he indicated towards the old man who had entered through the open doorway, "will bring you down when we have concluded our business," Mr. Red said.

The floorboards creaked as Patty and Mr. Kline clambered up the stairs to one of the smaller bedrooms.

"There you go, Miss."

After closing the door, Patty heard the distinct clink of a key turning in the lock. She tried the door. It was locked. *Paranoid military. Afraid she'd tiptoe downstairs and hear some secret shit.* Patty felt comforted knowing she was being taken care of by a friend of her fathers'.

\*\*\*

"That was a hokey excuse you used," Mr Gold said. "As if the North Vietnamese are going to send spies to track her down here and interrogate her."

"All I had to do was scare her so bad she'd believe anything. It worked didn't it. She's a kid. She's not going to question us," Mr. Red smiled.

"Captain," Mr. Gold said indicating with his hand for him to sit in the chair Patty had just vacated. "What can you report?"

"The Russian and Giap escaped through a hatch in the floorboards under Giap's desk."

Too many voices all at once made it impossible to determine who was saying what. "You were supposed to be the best," "We were counting on you," "What do you expect us to do now?" "For fuck sake!"

"And now you've given us another problem. And for what! With no results. What about Mr. ..." Mr. Gold couldn't think of his name.

"Tehrani, from—" supplied Mr. Red.

Mr. Gold was quick to cut him off. "Yes, what about him?"

The captain avoided their eyes and shook his head. "Killed."

"Money wasted. See, I told you we shouldn't have paid half up front." Mr. Gold's tongue snapped behind his teeth, making that annoyed sound. "Do you know why we call these operations covert?"

The captain ran his hand over the nape of his neck and remained quiet.

"This isn't a rhetorical question. I'm waiting," Mr. Gold said.

"Because it's top-secret."

"Yes. Does that mean anything to you? Why would you bring this woman with you when you know she shouldn't be witness to any of it?" Mr. Gold leaned in and stretched his chest over the table. His teeth were clenched, and his knuckles were pressed white against the table. "Do you know who this woman is?"

"A USO entertainer." The captain's scowl pinched his nose and stole his charm.

"She's a general's daughter. And guess who gave me this information? Her daddy's good friend Colonel Burke from the American Embassy in Saigon."

Sweat broke out on the captain's forehead.

"What if the colonel called his friend to tell him the good news? That his daughter is safe and on her way home." Mr. Gold was almost out of his seat.

Mr. Red interjected. "This woman is also an anti-war demonstrator. We have newsreel of her at Capitol Hill at a big sit-in. How do you propose we keep her quiet and...?"

Mr. Blue interrupted. "This is the kind of shit that can start WWIII. She's a bleeding heart and they don't change their color."

"Fucking bitch. I wanted to take her out, but Soko wouldn't let me."

Firmly planted in his seat again, Mr. Gold enunciated each word and thumped his fist on the table. "You were in charge?"

"I wanted to waste her before the climb."

"Keep your voice down." Mr. Blue got out of his chair. "No sense making matters worse."

Mr. Gold glowered at him. "The kitchen is soundproof."

"That was done years ago, who knows if it's still good." Mr. Blue sat down again.

"You don't trust anything," Mr. Gold said.

Mr. Blue glared at the captain. "I trusted him to get the job done."

"Soko started a mutiny and turned the men against me. I figured there was no point fighting Soko when she wouldn't make it off the mountain anyway."

"And yet, here she is." Mr. Gold's exaggerated hand movements matched his sarcasm.

"If it weren't for Soko, she wouldn't be here."

"Enough excuses," Mr. White said.

"Did you find proof that Russia agreed to supply nuclear weapons?"

The captain shook his head for no.

"Is this the level of expertise we can expect from you in the future?" Mr. Gold asked.

The captain gripped the edge of the table. "What about Soko …Sokoloski?"

Two others put their weight on it. Many a table had been overturned when tempers flared.

"One problem at a time. By letting Colonel Burke relay Miss Fielding's history to us, you have put us in an untenable situation," Mr. Gold said.

"I'll take care of Colonel Burke."

Mr. White ground out a cigarette in an ashtray. "That won't be necessary. Mr. Gold has already solved that problem. Killings and bombings are commonplace now in Saigon. Sometimes a lot of good men are lost."

"Miss Fielding is quite an attractive woman, wouldn't you say?" Mr. Gold studied the captain's body language.

"She's not my type."

"Have you met her father?"

"No."

"If you were us, how would you resolve this problem?"

The captain sat forward in his chair. "I'd slit the bitch's throat and dump her back in 'Nam."

"What if Colonel Burke contacted her father to let him know she was safe and on her way back to the USA?"

The captain shifted in his chair. "Guess, I'd have to kill the general too."

"That's quite the trail of bodies. Too many bodies create suspicion. The girl is already MIA and presumed dead. So, her corpse showing up in Vietnam is expected. Unfortunately, the Colonel could have verified that she is alive and headed here."

"Her father is the unknown variable in this equation. If Burke didn't contact her father, then as far as he's concerned, she's still MIA and probably dead."

"Then what's the problem?" the captain asked.

"What if Burke did tell him and the general knows she's alive? It's not like we can pick up the phone and ask him if he's heard from his daughter. Unless someone here knows him."

"I've seen him maybe twice at a meeting over ten years," Mr. White said. "But never spoken to him."

"Contacting the general or getting someone to contact him now would raise suspicion. I think we can all agree, we have to get rid of her. The only question is where her body should be found. Here or in Vietnam?" Mr. Gold scanned around the table at the heads nodding in agreement.

"We must know unequivocally that her father still believes she's MIA. For now, it's best to keep Miss Fielding sequestered. If he knows, she's returned, he will contact her. We have bugged her phone, his home, and his office phones. I think it's safe to assume if he hasn't contacted her within three days, then, he knows nothing of her return. Then our," he emphasized the word, "problem is solved."

"Is that why you brought her clothes? To make sure she was found dressed in clothes that belonged to her?" the captain asked.

"Yes, and also clothes that suit the climate. If we instruct you to take her to Vietnam, there are lightweight clothes appropriate for that climate. Make sure she doesn't use the phone in the cabin. We can't have her talking to her father or his receptionist."

\*\*\*

Patty was upstairs rummaging through her suitcase. Three bras, three underwear, enough clothes for three days. A man must have packed her things. No woman would mix in a summery sleeveless top and lightweight mini skirt with two pairs of blue jeans and winter sweaters. Changing into her blue jeans and thick red sweater, she heard the front door open and then close, and she wondered who was coming or going.

Feeling the comfort of being in her own clothes, she threw the army attire, provided by the embassy, over the back of a chair. Taking out the photograph, she slipped it into her blue jeans back pocket. Strange how they knew how many days of clothes to pack before speaking with her. Not knowing what to make of the whole situation, she was just happy it would be over in three days. The front door opened and closed again.

There was a knock on her door. The old man said, "Time to go."

He unlocked it and escorted her downstairs to the front hall where the captain was putting on a winter coat.

Mr. Gold handed her a winter coat and boots. "The captain will be your guard and escort now."

Patty scrutinized the captain. He smiled back.

Putting on her boots, she said, "Thank you for all your help. I appreciate it."

The old man opened the door and escorted them out.

The chauffeur handed the car keys to the captain. Patty settled into the passenger seat and closed the door.

"Where are we going?" she asked.

The captain turned the radio up and tuned her out. Patty preferred it that way. She didn't like or trust him. She was upset that she hadn't thought to ask whether Soko could guard her instead. Everything had happened so fast she didn't have time to think. But three and a half hours in the car with Mr. Personality had cleared her mind.

"How much longer?"

"About an hour. Maybe longer with this weather."

She thought she'd left the fear behind, but instead, she brought it along with her. Afraid to be in a cabin alone with him for three days, she hoped he could be trusted to obey orders. Closing her eyes, she tried to sleep.

Patty nodded in and out. She couldn't get comfortable. Or maybe it was the worry. They were coming up to a small town. Off the highway leading to the town, was a gas station. The captain drove over to the pump and asked the guy to "fill-her-up."

Entering the town, there were no stop lights, only a main street with old buildings that seemed to grow out of the ground. He pulled into a building parking lot with a sign that read groceries/liquor/beer. Patty noted the time. They'd have a couple of hours before it got dark.

The captain shut off the engine. "This is the last town before the cabin. We need food and supplies for three days."

Before entering the store, they stomped the snow off their boots. She wheeled the grocery cart while the captain filled it with a case of Rheingold beer and a bottle of whiskey from the window display. To anyone, they appeared to be a married couple, albeit a couple who weren't speaking to each other. Stopping in front of the canned soups, they each selected their three favorites. Patty picked out a jar of peanut butter while he chose jam. They walked up and down the aisles loading up pop, potato chips and other snacks, milk, a loaf of bread, and TV dinners. Patty chose chicken dinners while the captain went for the beef. She dropped a container of chocolate ice cream on top of the frozen dinners.

She was self-conscious waiting in line, aware of people's stares, feeling like a victim of spousal abuse. The captain didn't seem to notice, or maybe he just didn't want to acknowledge it. Pushing the cart out of the store, it left a trail of deep ruts in the snow to the trunk of the car. With the groceries loaded, the captain started the car, turned on the overhead light, and perused a map before handing it to Patty.

They headed out. It started snowing. They were the kind of snowflakes that hit the windshield head-on to give one a hypnotic feeling. Driving twenty-seven miles down a plowed paved road, the captain turned left onto an old dirt road. Its washboard ruts were layered in ice and snow.

Tree limbs weighted down with snow bowed over the edge of the road giving a closed-in feeling. Dense forests covered both sides of the road. Patty leaned her cheek against the cold glass window anticipating the swelling would go down.

"Sit up. Watch for deer," the captain ordered.

Patty stared out the window, ready to react if she spotted one. The captain accelerated up a hill, causing the car to slide sideways. Bracing her feet, her nails dug into the dashboard as the vehicle skated back and forth a few times before he managed to straighten it out.

\*\*\*

Soko watched the captain's car disappear down the other side of the hill. He had been pursuing them since they left the airport. He was glad he had trusted his gut. When doing surveillance, he knew to follow two car lengths behind. In the city, riding their tail in heavy traffic wasn't difficult since congestion prohibited speed.

Parked at the top of the street with a clear view of the sedan that was positioned behind four rusted, late-model cars opposite a dilapidated house looked suspicious. Especially since there were only two other vehicles on both sides of the streets. Washington was up to something. It didn't feel right. He was surprised they were there for so long. There was little that could be said about their failed mission. When the captain pulled out, Soko tailed him in his Mustang. Once they were outside the city and on the highway, the traffic picked up and cars wove in and out of lanes making it more difficult, with falling snow. Switching lanes prevented the captain from noticing his tail.

Parked across the street from the grocery store, he had taken out his binoculars from the glove box and observed them through the large storefront window. But now, being on the dirt road with no other vehicles made hiding difficult. He couldn't get too close.

After seeing the difficulty, the captain had going uphill, Soko was prepared for the slippery conditions and handled the car with ease. At the bottom of the hill, he bounced over a section of road that had heaved from frost. He stayed far behind, following their tracks rather than their car that could no longer be seen.

Driving along the white ribbon of road between trees and rock cuts, he stopped when the captain's car ahead slowed. Then it backed up and entered a side road. Soko's windshield wipers were iced up and left blurry streaks as they moved back and forth. His nose was close to the windshield. The tire tracks ahead stopped abruptly, with multiple tracks that backed up and down the nearby driveway. Steering the car to the side of the road, Soko checked the mileage from town and shut off the engine. He took his winter coat and wool knit cap out of its thermal blanket in the back seat of the car, put it on, and got out. There was a sign that said, "The Golds."

Thick evergreen trees lined both sides of the lane, obscuring the cabin from view. Wide swaths from a truck's plow were dusted by the newly fallen snow. The lane seemed like it had been plowed earlier that day. Bits of earth and stones dug up by the plow had pockmarked the snowbanks. *Long driveway. Good thing they didn't have to dig their way in.*

The captain had parked the car. Walking along the thicket of trees bordering the laneway, Soko saw the front door open and jumped back into the trees.

"Come here and give me a hand." the captain yelled from the front porch.

When Patty slammed the front door, snow slid off the porch roof. She looked up at it.

The captain tilted his head upward. "Hopefully it's strong enough to support the weight. It'd be a bitch up there, shoveling in this cold."

He punched at long icicles that hung from the edge of the roof, then pulled back a heavy canvas tarp that covered a generator and a pile of firewood. "It looks well-seasoned and ready to burn. Open the door and leave it open until we get the wood in."

Patty loaded her arms with logs and went into the cabin. After the wood had been hauled in, they unloaded the groceries from the trunk. Picking up the last two bags, Patty hesitated and stared into the trunk. She put the bags back in the trunk and rummaged through something before picking them up again and going back into the cabin.

Sneaking up to a window, Soko peered through the glass. Patty was putting groceries away while the captain was shoving logs into the firebox, scrunching paper around them. Bright flames shot up the chimney flue when he set the paper on fire. This domestic scene had him perplexed. He couldn't figure out why Washington wanted her hidden away. Why keep her away from her father? It made no sense. If Washington wanted her dead, the captain would have killed her. But with the ground frozen, he couldn't bury her. She'd have to be burned or chopped. But instead, he's buying groceries and building a fire. Strange. There were a lot of groceries. Enough for three or four days.

Soko ducked out of sight when the cabin door opened. He was tempted right then to grab Patty's hand and run to his car with her. But he had no weapon or plan. He watched her bury frozen dinners and ice cream beside the pop and milk.

If he broke into the cabin, he would have to kill the captain to get Patty. If Washington sent her here, then they would track her down. They wouldn't be safe anywhere. They needed help from someone with clout.

He needed to find out why she was sequestered and who was behind it. If they were keeping her away from her father, then the general was the person he needed to talk to. Besides, he was the only one who could be trusted with her life. He couldn't call. Washington was notorious for tapping phones. If Washington thought she was safely under wraps, then he was free to investigate. He would fly to Fort Benning.

# Chapter 18

The earliest flight from Reagan Airport wasn't until the next day. Soko arrived at Columbia, Georgia at ten a.m. Passing throngs of people waiting beside luggage conveyor belts, he spotted a car rental booth. When Soko rented a car and asked how he could get to Fort Benning, the accommodating clerk laid out a map and traced his three-and-a-half-hour route.

"Thanks," Soko said, taking the map and keys.

This traffic wasn't nearly as bad as in Washington. Soko studied the map and knew where he was going. He drove down Victory Dr and turned right down the I85 and crossed the bridge where the Chattahoochee River turned into Upatoi Creek. Coming out to First Division Road, he turned left on Yeager Ave. to the main post where he parked the car.

He assumed the general's office would be bugged so he would have to communicate with him in writing. Arranging an appointment would delay him. On the hotel stationary, last night, he had written: *Your office is bugged. Patty is alive in the USA but they are going to kill her. I was with her in Nam. She's daddy's little sharpshooter nicknamed Bullseye. Meet me at Ruby's Bar and Grill on 139 Victory Dr. Now.*

Soko had no trouble finding General Fielding's office. He walked to his secretary's desk in front of his closed door.

"How can I help you?" she asked.

"Is the general in?"

"Yes, but he's extremely busy. Do you have an appointment?"

"No." Soko held up the envelope containing his note. "But he'll want to be interrupted for this."

The secretary rolled her eyes. "You must wait your turn like everyone else. I can book you an appointment, but he won't be able to see you for a few days."

Reaching for a pen and the pad of paper on her desk he wrote: *His office is bugged. Don't be responsible for him leaking sensitive eyes-only information to an enemy? This could get you fired.* Soko handed her the paper and put his finger to his lips.

Flipping the sealed envelope from front to back, she hesitated. "The general is in an important meeting with high-level officials. I shouldn't interrupt him."

"All the more reason. This is urgent. He will thank you."

She turned away and knocked timidly on the door. The general stood in the doorway. Soko retreated behind a pillar. "I'm sorry," the secretary said, "I didn't know what to do." She handed him the envelope. "He said it was urgent."

General Fielding opened the envelope and read the note. "Bullseye, I haven't called her that in years," he said out loud. "Who gave you this?"

When the secretary turned around, Soko was gone. "A man. He didn't give his name."

"What did he look like?"

She gave him a description.

The general read the note again. "What color was his hair?"

"I don't know. He wore a jeep cap."

"Give my apologies to the men inside. Cancel the rest of my appointments for the day. I have no idea when I'll be back." He squeezed her shoulder. "You did the right thing."

∗∗∗

They met at Ruby's, in a back booth.

Sliding into the leather seat, the general said, "What's this about?"

Soko filled him in on everything including their mission.

Glancing over at the front door to make sure he wasn't followed, Soko asked, "Do you know Colonel Burke?"

"He's a long-time friend."

"When we got to the Saigon embassy, he took Patty's information and forwarded it on to Washington."

"If we could find out who he spoke to that would give us a lead. I'll call my secretary..."

"No, her phone might be bugged. They'd know we're on to them."

"Okay, I've got other sources."

"There's a phone booth at the back."

That was why Soko had chosen this place. The phone booth was secluded from the restaurant. They pooled their change. Soko straddled the telephone booth's doorframe while the general made calls. It took a while before the operator made the connection to the Saigon embassy.

The general held the receiver between them so they could both hear. "American embassy," the woman's voice at the other end said.

"Colonel Burke, please."

With the long silence, they stared at each other.

"Ah, um, I'm sorry sir. But I um...I hate to be the one to tell you, but he was killed yesterday."

Soko saw the shock on the general's face, and it took him a few seconds to recover to ask, "How?"

"Shot outside the embassy. In broad daylight."

"Did they get the shooter?"

Curious, Soko moved in closer.

"No. It's under investigation."

"What time was that?"

"I can transfer you through to Colonel Cathcart, he's taking over."

"No. That won't be necessary. What time was that again?"

The sound of dishes breaking on the linoleum distracted Soko.

"It was the afternoon because I heard about it after I got back from a late lunch."

"Thank you," he said and hung up.

The general's face had gone from pink to pale. "We have to get her out of there. They're going to kill her."

"Why would they kill her?"

"She's an anti-war demonstrator."

"No," Soko said. She's a USO entertainer."

"She wanted to see her brother—make sure he was alright. I never understood it." He put his head in his hands. "They were close—maybe too close." His fingers spread when he used them to massage his forehead. "She was like a mother hen to him. Even when they were kids. It got worse after her mother died. But she's against the war and protests all the time."

"Damn it. I knew I should have gotten her out when I had the chance. You're right. If they know she's a protestor, they'll kill her. But why would she go into a combat zone if she was against the war?"

The general shrugged at him. "I guess, it doesn't matter. She did it for her brother."

"They'll kill her. Doves are the enemy at home. With the army, an enemy is an enemy regardless of where they are. They can't trust her to keep their secret."

"I'm going to get her," the general said.

"Once we have her, we have to get her out of the country fast."

"Are you going with her?"

"Yes." Soko hadn't hesitated.

"I can get passports, social security cards, driver's licenses, all your ID under false names. I have to get back to my office to put everything in motion. It will take two days maybe longer. Where are you staying?"

Soko wrote down the name, phone number, address of the motel, and his room number and handed it to him.

The general gave Soko his home address and home phone number. "Ring once then hang up, so I know it's you. I'll get to a secure line and call you back at your motel. Stay put until you hear from me."

\*\*\*

It was two days later at eight in the morning, when Soko got the call from the general. He would be there as soon as he could. Soko was to be ready.

Get ready—the general's words stuck in his head. How could he get ready for his life to be changed forever? That had kept him awake the last two nights. The military was everything he had ever wanted—everything he had worked so hard for. It was his career, his way of life that he thought would be forever. The politician's deceit had taken integrity out of the job. He couldn't remain loyal to them or the military.

He loved his country, and the reality of having to leave it and his life with his family was painful. He was torn. Not between the decision of helping Patty and betraying the politicians, but by the loss—of no family, no country, no identity, and no life-long plans realized.

When the general arrived, he escorted Soko to the rental agency where he could return his vehicle. Then Soko opened the general's car door and slid into the passenger seat.

"Where are we going?"

"Lawson Army Airfield. A chopper is fueled up and ready for us. I have a pilot waiting."

"Can he be trusted?"

"We go back to infantry days in the trenches. He watched Patty grow up. He'd do anything for her. She's the closest he has to a daughter."

They took Dixon Road to Jecelin Road to get to the airfield. As expected, the pilot and chopper were on the tarmac. The general drove up to the chopper.

"Bill this is Paul." The general introduced Soko by his new name.

Opening his trunk, the general and Soko unloaded duffle bags. Getting back into the car, the general drove to a second hangar, parked, and walked back to the men. They boarded the helicopter and were airborne in no time. The general opened the largest of the duffle bags. He gave Soko a .38-caliber revolver with ammo. He put the .45 automatic pistol on the seat beside him.

"I brought the grease gun for you Bill. I've seen your scores at the range."

"Eyesight isn't what it used to be. Getting old, I guess." Bill leaned out of his seat and took note of the grease gun and ammo the general put on the floor behind the co-pilot's seat. It was a blowback submachine gun that was fired on automatic—small and lightweight.

"I've got my .45 too," Bill said.

"We don't need to see it. Both hands on the controls," Soko said.

"Cyclic," Bill corrected him.

"I don't care what they're called. I only know it takes both hands and both feet to fly."

"A little skittish, isn't he?" Bill said.

The general didn't reply.

"It's been a while since I was in a skirmish. Good thing for Thursday's firing range practices." Bill adjusted his hand on the cyclic.

Two sacks of ammo were left in the duffle bag.

"I feel better seeing the firepower," Soko said. "When was the last time you fired one of these?"

Stuffing his pockets with more ammo, the general scowled at Soko.

Bill stepped in to defend him. "The general was a sniper. He's trained more snipers than any other at base. You wait and see. He'll turn Fort Benning into a sniper school. In his prime, he was the best of the best. His idea of family time was spent at the firing range. Patty couldn't get enough of it. She's like him."

The second duffle bag contained maps, toiletries, a couple of family photographs, and a briefcase with Soko and Patty's ID.

The general's features softened as he handed the briefcase to Soko. "I know you're just watching out for my daughter, and I appreciate it."

Two hours were spent exchanging information.

"The cabin is two hundred and seventy-nine miles from Raegan Airport," Soko said.

The general got out a map of Washington D.C. and the area. "Show me on the map," he said handing Soko a red pen.

"When you reach this town," he circled it on the map, "It is exactly thirty-three miles to the cabin. It's on a dirt road five point seven miles from the paved one." He circled the location in red, then sketched out a detailed layout of the inside and outside of the cabin.

"We can't go busting into the cabin. The captain will use Patty as a shield. Shoot through a window." He regretted not taking the shot through the window when the captain had been building the fire. He'd been an easy target. But then where would they have gone? How could they have protected themselves? They wouldn't have lasted long. The military would have made sure they wouldn't reach the general.

He tried to reassure himself that he'd made the right decision but worried that he'd left her alone for too long.

Soko opened the briefcase and rummaged through his ID. "It could fool anyone."

"The benefits of rank. It looks official, because it is. With my clearance, I have access to things like this."

Soko closed the briefcase. "The chopper is loud. How can we surprise the captain? The generator isn't loud enough to mask the sound of a chopper."

Bill shouted back, "I can fly low to the ground, downwind, and avoid taking sharp angles. But I wouldn't want to land any closer than three miles away."

"So, about an hour's walk." the general said.

"Yeah, that's about right," Bill agreed.

The general moved up into the co-pilot's seat to give Bill the coordinates when they flew over Washington D.C.

Soko was relieved when they were out of the city and into the heavily wooded area. He remembered buildings, farms, silos, and scenery along the way. The general steered Bill to the paved road. It had been plowed and the trees didn't bow as much as they had when they were ladened with snow. They were getting closer.

"There's the grocery store." Soko pointed out below. He recognized the hill down below where he had skidded after the turnoff onto the dirt road.

"Okay, it's not much farther." Bill checked the flight instruments. "This is the closest I want to get, but there's no place to land except on the road. So, hang on. It could be a little bumpy."

Soko braced his feet. After they landed, Bill shut off the engine. They waited a few minutes for the rotors to decelerate.

Bill unbuckled his seat belt. "Don't worry. Patty can handle herself. She's a spitfire, just like her old man."

The general closed his eyes and wiped a tear before it could roll down his cheek. "I know. She's my little sharpshooter." His voice cracked.

# Chapter 19

The cabin was cool as the fire had dwindled during the night. Coming out of his bedroom, the captain sauntered into the living room and stoked the embers, adding newspaper and kindling. He blew into the firebox. Within a short time, flames shot up around the paper and licked the logs. A cozy heat pushed into the room to warm the cold wooden floor.

Patty awoke and got dressed. The thick green sweater felt cool from sitting on the dresser.

Last night, when she went into the freezer to get ice cream, there was one beef TV dinner left. *One for him and none for me? With no dinner for me, this has to be the last day. Should I pack my suitcase? The phone never rang, so the captain hadn't received further instructions.*

Patty hated talking to the captain and had curled into a corner reading books for the last couple of days. This was the third day of their confinement. After today, she had no more clean underwear. She felt something was going to change today but didn't know what. Except that she wouldn't be here for dinner.

She smelled toast and dreamed about peanut butter to go with it. When she walked into the kitchen, she wasn't taken aback to see the captain drinking a bottle of beer. That seemed to be his morning routine. Treading carefully by him, she said nothing. Patty took two slices of bread out of the loaf he had left open on the counter and dropped them into the toaster. When her toast popped up, she layered it with peanut butter, poured herself a glass of milk, and headed toward the fire to curl up in the over-stuffed chair. After finishing breakfast, she cleaned the dishes and then went to the bathroom. The door didn't lock. She wouldn't take a shower because of that.

The front door of the cabin opened, and she felt a draft beneath the bathroom door. She ran out hoping it was her dad, but it was just the captain going outside. Disappointed, she headed to her bedroom to get a blanket. Taking a book from the double-sided bookcase that divided the kitchen from the living room, she stepped aside when the captain came in with another armload of firewood.

Wrapped in a blanket, she plopped into the chair near the fireplace and read. He sat at the kitchen table and played solitaire. His beer and the whiskey bottle were within easy reach. Patty was up to Chapter Seven, but it was a slow go. She was distracted by the number of times he opened the fridge and got another beer.

It was almost time for lunch and her last can of vegetable soup. He got up and moved toward her in the chair. Lifting a handful of hair at the nape, his hot breath touched her skin.

"Cherry intact," he teased. "Nothing like a sweet cherry," he licked her neck.

Patty turned around fast, whipping hair out of his grasp, and jumped out of the chair.

"Ring-a-ding-ding. Time for a fling." He leaned back into a laugh.

She ran to the fireplace and picked up the poker.

*Had to be a smart ass. Couldn't leave it alone. Stupid! Payback always backfires.*

Goose bumps rose on Patty's arms. She noticed the wall-mounted phone in the living room next to the door. His head turned in that direction too.

He chimed again, "Ring-a-ding-ding," Lips curling into a smirk, he strolled away and settled into the brown leather recliner opposite her.

She dropped the poker onto the hearth, settled back into the chair, and tucked into the blanket. *Time for a fling!* Those words invaded each paragraph she read. *He was drunk. Drunk people tell the truth. What was that large black zippered bag in the trunk for? A body bag? Was it the chauffeur's or did someone from the safehouse put it in the trunk? Someone had gone out and come in. I heard the door that night. Now you're imagining some psycho scene. Stop it. The chauffeur could have had that for any reason. A garment bag for his uniform! Of course.* She laughed. *OMG, you're losing it. Stop being melodramatic! He's drunk and he's an asshole. He still has to obey orders.*

The last two afternoons, after lunch, the captain had leaned back in the recliner with feet up. He drank until he was too tired to stay awake. It amazed Patty that he didn't nod off holding the bottle. He had the timing down. Just before he fell asleep, he leaned over the arm of the chair and lined up the empty beer bottle on the floor with the others.

It was the only time Patty could relax. The whisky bottle sat on the end table beside the recliner. Beer was the chaser for the whisky. She knew how angry some men could get when they drank. And she didn't want to find out if he was that type.

She got up to put another log on the fire. The phone rang and startled the captain from his nap. Jumping up from the lounger, he stumbled over, and answered it. Patty watched his groggy expression change to a wide smile. She knew from his silence; he was being given instructions. The captain stood between her and the door. He ogled her, with his mouth wide open, tongue stuck out. He flicked it up and down.

*Ring-a-ding-ding, Time for a fling!*

Patty almost overturned the chair when she leaped out of it. Picking up the poker, she ran to the kitchen. Yanking open the cutlery drawer, she pulled out a butcher knife and then into the bedroom. She knew enough not to bother with the bars on her window. She'd tried to pry them out earlier with a butter knife, but it hadn't worked.

Dragging the long heavy dresser in front of the door, she barricaded herself in. But if she could move it, so could he. She shoved the heavy wooden bedframe and bed against the dresser. Hefting the two nightstands, she put them on top of the dresser along with her suitcase. She could hear his boots thumping along the floor.

"It's just you and me. This could be an afternoon of R and R and a lot of FU."

The footsteps were getting closer. Patty knelt on the bed brandishing the weapons. The door nob turned.

He thrust against the door. "Now don't spoil our fun."

Patty shrieked.

"No one can hear you. There's nothing, and no one's around."

He charged into the hardy batten and ledged frame construction and jostled the barrier of furniture. The door opened a bit. His arm reached into the room. She beat it with the poker.

He yelled, "Fucking bitch, goddamn whore!" Then he laughed, and his tone changed to mocking. "I forgot you're a virgin."

Taking another run at the door, he slammed his shoulder into the wood. "Ahh." He shouted holding his arm in pain.

"I'm going to ram it to you. I got a boner already. Don't know if I've ever had a virgin. Yup. It's your lucky day."

The hand that held the knife shook. The screams reverberating off the walls were even more frightening when they echoed back at her.

He banged and thumped on the door, dislodging the furniture. "I'm coming for you bitch." His words spit through the opening.

Patty pushed back, but all that furniture was too heavy to budge. "Mr. Gold will court-martial you."

His laugh was terrifying. "Mr. Gold ordered me to kill you. Tomorrow we're going back to Nam. Except just one of us will be enjoying the view."

Tears streamed down her cheeks, and she snuffled back her runny nose. "You're wrong. Mr. Gold is a friend of my father's."

"He gave me the body bag in the trunk. You'll be nice and stiff when we fly back to 'Nam. With this weather, it'd be like being in a freezer. You'll thaw quick in 'Nam though. Nothing worse than the stink of a dead body."

"Mr. Gold will kill you."

"Mr. Gold doesn't like chicken shit, anti-war demonstrators. And neither do I."

The men at the safehouse were the only ones who could have told him she was a protestor. They were in on this with him! She screeched long and hard until she winded herself. His boot kicked the door rattling it.

Doubled over, panting to catch her breath, Patty heard the front door open. Then it was quiet. As soon as she had enough air, she hollered again. Her body shuddered so badly it vibrated the poker. Too heavy to hold, she laid it on the bed beside her. His boots pounded the wooden floorboards.

The captain was at the door again, his voice like a sing-song chant. "Washington cut down a cherry tree and I'm going to get me a cherry too." The axe splintered the door.

Patty picked up the fire iron off the bed. "I've got a poker and I'm going to take your head off."

"Ah now, why would you do that? And here I'm going to dress you up pretty in those summer clothes of yours."

She heard him grunt as he swung the axe over his shoulder. The blade sliced through the bedroom door. She saw his face leering at her through the opening he made.

"Okay, so maybe you won't be so pretty after I throw you out of the chopper."

She watched as he brought the axe back.

The crack was loud. But the noise hadn't been from the door. The sound had come from the .38-caliber in the hand of the man standing behind the captain, visible now from behind her attacker through the splintered bedroom door.

Soko.

The force of the bullet's impact threw the captain against the door buckling it. Soko pulled his body off the door and let him fall to the floor. The general ran through the front door and put a bullet in the captain's head.

"Patty, it's Dad. It's Daddy, sweetheart." The general shouted over her cries. "Daddy's here."

"Daddy, is that really you?"

"Yes, I'm here."

"Stand back," Soko said.

She watched the two kick in and smash the remnants of the door, flinging chunks of wood into the living room. They threw the nightstands and pushed the dresser out of the way along with the bed. Patty dropped the poker. When they walked into the room, she fell into her father's arms, crying. He held her, rocking back and forth as tears lay in the creases around his eyes.

Her body trembled against his. He sat her on the bed, stroking her back until the tremors subsided. Then he asked. "Do you know who the captain was taking his orders from?"

"Mr. Gold. He said he was a friend of yours."

"Did you meet him?"

"Yes."

"What did he look like?"

When she gave him the description, he said, "It could be anyone."

"They were at a house."

"I know where the house is," Soko said.

Patty wiped her tears. "He said you were in Cambodia." Tears started again.

"It's alright."

"They were supposed to protect me."

Soko walked back through the gap they had made in the doorframe. She saw him bend down rifling through the captain's pockets. He pulled out car keys and a business card. He ambled away and returned, climbing through the doorframe. Side-stepping the mess, he handed her a wad of toilet paper.

"Wipe your eyes and blow your nose," he said.

Soko handed the general the elegantly printed, high-quality business card. Patty saw the name, Mr. Gold, and a phone number. It was the only printing on it.

After blowing her nose, she balled up the tissue. "I'm alright now."

"Okay, time to go," the general said, wrapping his arm around her back. Walking through the battered doorway, Patty contemplated the captain and the round exit wound between his eyes. His mouth was open, and his eyes were wide from shock. Blood pooled around him.

"Get your boots on." Her father retrieved her suitcase.

Soko pulled the keys out of his pocket. "I'll start the car."

Puffs of smoke billowed out the exhaust and the windshield and windows had been scraped clean when they walked out the front door and into the car. Soko drove a short distance before she saw a chopper parked on the road.

"Is that Uncle Bill?"

"Yup. You had to know he'd come with us."

Soko slowed the car, inching toward the chopper.

"He won't know it's us," the general said.

When the car stopped in front of the chopper and they all got out, Patty could see the relief on Bill's face.

The general waved. "Come, and give us a hand, Bill."

Together, they pushed the car off the road and into the trench. Clambering into the chopper, they buckled up.

Patty rubbed Bill's shoulder. "Thanks. Your timing has always been good, but this time it was perfect. You saved me, Uncle Bill."

He started the engine. "This sounds like a story I don't want to hear."

"I was surprised, for an old guy, you kept pace with me through the woods," Soko said to the general.

"Every time I heard Patty bawl, my legs almost buckled. The sound was like a blow. But the quiet twisted my gut. It was a relief to hear her scream again. I've survived battles and buried a wife, but nothing was as terrifying as this."

Bill swiveled behind him. "Don't think this old heart of mine could have taken that."

"She's safe and sound now." The general kissed his daughter on the cheek.

Patty hugged him back. "How did you know where to find me?"

"Your friend here." He thumped Soko on the chest. "I see you've become a pretty good judge of character after all."

Patty turned to Soko. "But how did you know?"

"At the airport. It didn't seem right that your dad wasn't there. So, I followed the car to the cabin. I knew I'd need some help. So, I enlisted your dad."

"Filthy bastards, they are. Manipulating and killing to get what they want." The general kept his eyes on Patty. "Authorized cruelty. Doesn't matter how innocent the people are."

"Yeah, but they're good at covering it up or classifying everything," Soko said.

"I knew some of this was going on, but it was easier to turn a blind eye to it. It's different when their tactics hit home. Colonel Burke was one of the good guys. And Patty..." Tears pooled in his eyelashes.

"I don't understand why I was a threat," Patty said. "I don't even know what the mission was about."

"They didn't know that. And it didn't matter that the mission failed. Look at the Bay of Pigs. People will be talking about that one for years. They couldn't take the chance that you'd go to the press. You were a protestor. The enemy. Not someone to be trusted."

"Airport's up ahead," Bill nodded. He brought the helicopter down in a smooth landing. They waited until the rotors stopped turning and then got out. Bill refueled.

"I need you two to go with Bill. He's going to take you to Toronto Canada. It's easier to get lost in a big city," the general said. He handed Patty an envelope. "There's eight-thousand dollars in it. Split it between the two of you. It will be easier to get through customs that way."

Patty saw the smirk on Soko's face. "You're coming with me?"

"Someone has to. You get into too much trouble on your own."

Replacing the fuel nozzle, Bill walked back to the group.

"Can you bring me the paperwork?" the general asked. Bill nodded and marched to the chopper.

"I have forms for you to fill out, and Bill will be the witness to make me your power of attorney since you won't be able to access your bank accounts. When you get new bank accounts set up in Canada, I'll close off the old accounts here and forward your money to you. After a time, when it seems like I've given up on Patty's return, I'll go to your apartments, pack up your things and send them to you."

Patty wasn't dumbfounded that her father had thought of all these things. He was a problem-solver.

Bill returned with the paperwork. They used the top of Soko's briefcase as a desk to sign the documents.

"I appreciate this." Soko set the case down on the pavement. "The faster we can disappear, the better."

"My sentiments exactly," the general agreed. "I know what it's like to be young and in love."

Patty cocked her head toward Soko and wondered what he had told her dad. He just shrugged his shoulders.

Patty didn't know whether they were in love. They didn't know each other well enough. But she wouldn't let on to her dad. Let him think what he wanted. In his day, love was a man committing to a woman. *I guess he figured by Soko giving up his career and country it meant he was ready for marriage.*

*I hope Dad's right. It could be love. Hard to tell, after only days together. And especially considering it was an intense time. Emotions were in high gear and accelerating. I'll see where it goes.*

Patty smiled, kissed her dad on the cheek, and hugged him.

*I saw that look. God forbid they should live in sin. How many times had I heard — Why buy the cow when you can get the milk for free?*

"I love you too, Bullseye."

The two clung to each other. "It's time to go." With a peck on the cheek, she was nudged toward Soko. "At least now, I know she'll be taken care of, and safe. Keep an eye on my little sharpshooter."

Soko saluted him and took Patty's hand to walk towards the chopper. They waved goodbye when Bill was cleared for take-off. The two in the back seat had so much to tell each other and get caught up on each other's lives. The surreal nature of their situation dissipated quickly when they heard Bill relaying information to a man in the radio tower at Toronto Pearson International Airport.

After landing in Canada, Patty kissed and hugged Bill goodbye. She and Soko walked hand-in-hand to the customs and immigration lineup. Their passports and declaration forms cleared inspection and life could begin again.

\*\*\*

I can't believe fifty-five years have passed. My life is disappearing. There are only a few boxes stacked and bits of furniture waiting for the moving van. It only took three months to clear out over half a century of memories. Pondering the back cover of *The Pentagon Papers*, I think of Daniel Ellsberg. He risked a maximum jail sentence of one hundred and fifteen years for espionage, theft, and conspiracy for releasing these papers. I thought of his interview on June 23rd 1971, hosted by Walter Cronkite on C.B.S.

Ellsberg felt President Johnson's reaction to him releasing these documents as being close to treason. It was very close to saying "I am the state." Alluding to a democracy changed to a dictatorship. I wondered if other presidents since had felt similarly—like they *were* the state.

Even Ellsburg said something about the ability of this country to keep secrets had gotten too good for our good. I remembered the secret I kept growing up in Fort Benning. It was a secret everyone knew but no one spoke about. Our neighbor Paula Noseworthy had constant black eyes and a split lip whenever her husband was home. I heard Paula's quiet sobs from my father's study. I hated her husband but kept his secret and knew my dad did too.

It wasn't right to keep that secret and it's not right to keep our secret now. Our children should at least know our real names. Maybe that's why I wrote much of my journal in the third person. So, I could write our real names. So, our children would know who we were and what we did.

I'm still the same person no matter what name I carry. Our girls know their aunts, uncles, and grandparents. We lied to keep the secret, telling our children that Soko (*oh, I mean Paul was adopted*). That accounted for the different last names. And my dad called me Bullseye.

I tucked the discolored photograph of me on stage into my journal. Picking up Soko's Zippo lighter, I read those faded words. "Morality is a choice." He lived life by those words. Our girls saw that in him. I turned it over and read the inscription he had put on the rear—Soko and Bullseye.

Since we both stopped smoking decades ago, I was surprised he still kept it, but was glad he had. It was a tangible thing to make our experience real to our kids. I opened an oversized purse and put these things into it along with *Defining the Times Magazine* and *The Pentagon Papers*. I wouldn't trust these treasures to the movers.

Now that I'm old, I don't want those memories of Vietnam to disappear, as if they hadn't happened. I want to reclaim our names and memories. I need our children and grandchildren to know the truth. I have a legacy to leave behind. Since Soko's death, I've been plagued by this. But it seems our girls are too busy with their lives to make time for the past.

I'm tired of recognizing names in the obituary section. Tired of proving I haven't lost it. Content to be led into the retirement home. It doesn't take long to settle down. There's not much left of my life now. A year goes by slowly in a prisoner's room, with a routine not to be messed with. Lying awake and listening for the ambulance that usually comes nightly, I wonder who it will be tonight and when it will be my turn. I think about my better half, wondering whether he waited for me to make myself whole again.

# Acknowledgements

Thank you to my publisher Shane Joseph who made my first experience working with a publisher a wonderful collaboration. His insightful guidance and ideas brought out the best of my book and made for an easy teamwork relationship.

Thank you, Terrie Frankel, for allowing me to use your picture from when you were a USO entertainer in 1968 Vietnam. For Terrie and her twin sister, Jennie, to have risked their lives at such a young age to entertain the troops was courageous. I salute you Terrie, Lifetime Honorary Commander of the 944th Fighter Wing, Luke Air Force Base. Terrie received the President's Award for Excellence in the Arts from the Vietnam Veterans of America. A truly giving person with credits as a New York Times bestselling author, musician, writer, composer, and producer.

Thank you, Matthew Connelly for your insightful book, *The Declassification Engine*, which helped me form this fictional novel into a more believable storyline. The information you have gathered through declassified documents is shocking. And must be read, to be believed.

Thank you to my editor friend, Margery Reynolds, for her many suggestions and corrections to improve the book and for finding me a qualified mountain climbing expert.

Thank you to Allison Rose, an expert climbing instructor, who helped me construct the climbing scenes.

Thank you to Darlene Roos who inspired me to take this book to the next level.

Thank you to a wonderful group of people from my Canadian Authors Association, Niagara Branch who critique my work, offering suggestions and corrections.

# Author Bio

Janice Barrett is a mother of three. Her children are her proudest accomplishments. She is a journalist, playwright and ghost writer. She gave a seminar at The Niagara Falls Literary Festival in 2018 on How to Write a Memoir. She spoke at Canada's Coast to Coast Tenacious Women's Literary Series at the Laura Secord Homestead.

Printed in the USA
CPSIA information can be obtained
at www.ICGtesting.com
LVHW010631280923
759525LV00039B/366